Darkness on the Nile

H. M. Gooden

Published by H. M. Gooden, 2019.

DARKNESS ON THE NILE

First edition. May 29, 2019.

Copyright © 2019 H. M. Gooden.

ISBN: 978-1989156148

Written by H. M. Gooden.

Also by H. M. Gooden

Standalone
The Raven and the Witch Hunter Omnibus: Volumes 2-4
To Capture the Heart of Spring
Darkness on the Nile

Watch for more at https://www.hmgoodenauthor.com/.

This book goes out to the beauty of ancient cultures and the lands they sprang up in.

I love researching my books almost as much as I enjoy writing them. Egypt is a country with such a fascinating history I think one needs to see it to be able to appreciate it fully.

There, myths and legends feel real in a way they don't anywhere else I've traveled.

I can't wait to see it again someday.

Prologue

B reathing hard, Naunet surveyed the damage. The once peaceful island in the middle of the Nile was strewn with debris from the activities of the night. Although shaky, she was otherwise unharmed, which is more than she could say about her enemies. Suddenly remembering her friends, she whirled, flipping her tail in the water to spin easily in a full 360 degrees as she searched for them.

She breathed out in relief when she spotted Robin on land, looking as mischievous as always, if slightly filthy. Olukun was...where was she? Even as her panic began to mount, her beautiful friend surfaced with a splash, her shiny black hair and tail glinting in the moonlight with a face as serene as ever.

They'd done it. They'd defeated them and had all come away from the battle unscathed. A tingle of happiness grew in her chest as Olukun approached, but it dampened instantly when her friend spoke.

"They are gone, for now." She intoned the words with a grim and an almost hollow echo that told Naunet more surely than anything else could have that her friend had seen the truth of the future.

"What do you mean, for now?" Naunet was pretty certain she knew what Olukun meant, but she wasn't ready to accept it yet.

Olukun turned, her profile a sharp contrast to the ruins of the outpost, which had served as a lookout until Kek and

Kauket had attempted their overthrow. She stared at it for several long moments while Naunet's apprehension mounted; then without turning to face her, Olukun answered, her voice once again calm.

"Darkness and light will always have a balance. If the bringer of the night and the bringer of the light were truly vanquished, the world would end. But with their greedy actions, they have overstepped their roles and tried to take on powers not meant for them to wield. By using humans as servants for such perversion, they have changed the magic, tarnishing it in a way that was never meant to be."

Naunet shuddered, recalling the awful things she'd seen in the weeks leading up to this fight. The bodies of humans controlled by the dead; Kauket's depraved glee in all things dark and evil. She couldn't say she regretted her own actions, even if she'd had to use her magic more offensively than ever before. She knew they'd stopped an immeasurable, world-altering evil tonight. She searched her friend's face, praying to the all-creator she had an answer.

"If it isn't over, what are we supposed to do? I can see no trace of either of them."

It was true. With the combined forces of Robin on land, controlling earth magic for their side, Olukun bringing her power of light and premonition, and Naunet being the equal of either of her brothers and sisters in origin and might, they'd been more than a match for the King and Queen of Darkness.

From the instant Olukun had lit up the night as bright as the day, there had been no sight of either of the gods.

Olukun shook her head, turning to Naunet with a reassuring smile. "Do not worry. When I say they aren't gone, I don't mean we'll need to face them again now or anytime soon. Balance is important though, and I believe you will again confront this magic once it has had sufficient time to regroup. Do not let your guard down—it will return when you least expect it."

Chapter 1

Naunet took her time swimming up the mouth of the Nile, a strange uneasiness holding her back from her normal carefree attitude. A faint disturbance in the water earlier that day had caused her to swim closer to shore than she had in a while.

Perhaps humans had succeeded in destroying the ecosystem after all, she thought sadly, watching as a can of flotsam passed by.

She'd been staying in the depths of the ocean for years now, hardly roaming away from the abyssal zone where she'd lived for centuries. As magic faded from the world and humans continued their seemingly inexorable advances into every space they could find, it had become harder for her to sit back and watch the destruction.

Once, the ocean had been pure and the land majestic as far as she could see. Now, plastic bottles competed with her for a space in the muddy waters of the Nile, and she couldn't even bear to think about what was happening above the surface.

The water became warmer the closer she swam to land and Naunet passed bright fish, including a few predators, without concern. She was ruler in this element with nothing to fear from any of her marine subjects. As the goddess of the deep oceans, she held sway over all the creatures dwelling within them and controlled water in a way others could not. But for the first time she could remember as she followed the water into the mouth of the Nile, a faint trickle of magic from nearby caused her heart to race.

A magic which she hadn't felt in a long time and had hoped never to feel again.

Maybe I'm wrong. But what if I'm not?

Even though she didn't want to be right, Naunet allowed the tingle to guide her forward. It became stronger as the river branched. Surfacing a few inches at a time, she paused to watch the sun dip into the west then glanced around for the source of the magic.

The usually busy shipping lanes were oddly silent tonight, and nothing stood out. Her trepidation increasing, she pressed her lips together and slipped beneath the smooth silk of the Nile. As she followed the disturbance further inland despite all her reservations, she trailed the stream of power as if she was the water version of a bloodhound. By the time she reached the location from where she felt it emanating from, the sky was dark and the stars were high.

If anyone had chanced to look toward the flat-bottomed Nile barge she was examining, they'd have seen what appeared to be a local girl out for a swim beside a pleasure cruiser. Unless they were perceptive enough to realize her hair and skin weren't the right shade to be human.

Without a sound, she slid up to the boat, avoiding the lights on the back. Stopping just out of range of their glow, she moved near enough to watch as a small group of people in the open center of the boat mingled. Unobserved by the partygoers, she was able to see eight people, two of whom she swiftly ruled out when she noticed they wore matching clothing. Uniforms.

The remaining six she examined more carefully but saw nothing of concern. Then, something shifted. The tingle of magic came again, this time more insistently and with more force as a tall man with dark hair and a neatly trimmed black beard entered her line of sight.

He wasn't one of the people she'd seen on the boat at first glance. He appeared to have just exited a small room at the back of the boat and joined the group of revelers. Outwardly, he looked like an average human in his twenties, perhaps as old as thirty. Guessing the age of humans wasn't her strength.

When she focused on him specifically, the same dark energy she'd sensed from afar was coming directly from him in dark waves, like plumes of black in water.

She wasn't a gifted aura reader, like some of her friends, but she was old and powerful in her own right. Her experience allowed her to see the magic contained within others, especially when it was a magic she'd hoped had been lost to humans forever. Magic that would wreak unimaginable evil upon the world if it were allowed to return.

Naunet sank back down in the water until she was completely submerged. Running a hand through long, chartreuse hair, she rubbed her neck in a vain attempt to relieve the tension caused by what she'd seen. Her magic was powerful, but she knew her limitations, the largest which was weakness when she was far from her element. Egypt, while the closet country to the depths she called home, had the least water of anywhere she'd traveled.

Naunet was flooded by memories of the last time she'd felt this dark magic and her weakness then in the face of what she'd seen. If it hadn't been for the help of her friends, she wouldn't be here now. Apprehension grew alongside her surprise and disappointment as she thought about that experience.

Once, many years ago, humans had discovered the power of necromancy. Even now, she was unsure how it had come to pass, only that it had been due to the actions of her own kind. Once they had begun to use it though, they'd been willing and reckless. For the first time, even humans without their own gifts could channel the powers of the gods.

They had gone far beyond what was wise, twisting magic beyond what nature had intended. They greedily brought back their beloved dead, then had gone even further. High priests had taken the information gleaned from Kek and Kauket and learned how to trap the powers of a god within the frail shell of a human. By binding their magic in a vessel they controlled, the priests could then harness the power of their prisoner to use as if it was their own. A shudder ran through her at the remembered profanity.

I will not allow it to happen again.

For the first time in centuries, Naunet steeled herself. She had to involve herself in human affairs now, no matter what the personal cost. As the river boat drifted lazily along the Nile into the night and the humans on board readied themselves for sleep, Naunet watched, biding her time.

Chapter 2

By the time the sun rose over the Nile the next morning, Naunet had been following the boat for over eight hours. She was tired, despite her magic, and wanted nothing more than to sleep. But sleep was a luxury she couldn't afford. At least not until after the boat docked and she had a chance to find out what the dark stranger was up to. So when the boat stopped in Luxor, she let out a huge sigh of relief.

Unobserved, Naunet slid between the luxury cruiser she'd been following and another boat, waiting until the people she'd seen on deck exited as a group. She swiftly slipped on board, transforming with a shimmer into her land form. While her hair remained a greenish-yellow, a shade darker than her moss-green skin, at least her figure appeared human.

Without delay, she headed to the ship's hold where extra uniforms would be kept aboard sailing vessels such as this one. She secured a uniform she'd found which fit reasonably well, then turned to catch up with the group and nearly ran into a startled elderly man.

He had white hair, a clean-shaven face, and stood gaping at her in the doorway, his eyes scanning her unusual coloring with confusion. He wore a uniform similar to the one she'd borrowed, and she gave him her most brilliant smile as she bobbed her head deferentially.

"Sorry. I forgot something." She smiled again, this time adding a trickle of power. Satisfaction filled her as his expression melted into one of warm acceptance. He smiled back, his confusion replaced by a placid contentment.

She brushed past the man without saying anything more, knowing he was watching her leave. He wouldn't cause a scene now that he'd been captivated by her beauty and glamor. She focused on her skin, having forgotten until she'd seen his expression that her natural color wasn't remotely human.

Using his dark olive skin as a template, she checked her arms to make sure she'd achieved a more realistic shade then went aboveboard, striding down the narrow gangplank and pausing on the boardwalk beside the river. To her relief, she heard the same voices of the group from the boat chattering only a hundred feet away.

Luxor was a place most humans dreamed of seeing one day. From the sounds of this bunch, they'd come from far away in order to experience the wonders of Egypt. Naunet smiled wistfully, thinking about how simple being human would be. To find joy in things older than you were, appreciating the time you had with your short life span while never realizing how much had been destroyed because of your ancestors.

The library in Alexandria was a perfect example. Although tourists still flocked to see it, the first one had truly been the wonder of the world. She could still remember its magnificence. Standing as it had against the backdrop of the Mediterranean Sea, she'd visited often. When Naunet thought of all the knowledge lost that day so long ago, she was still devastated. But perhaps humans weren't meant to know the entirety of what had been archived within those halls and it was all for the best. Knowledge of things such as the dark magic she could smell ahead of her.

Maybe the gods themselves had caused that long-ago destruction, not the careless humans who seemed to love playing with fires they couldn't begin to control. Sighing, she forced her thoughts back to the present danger and hurried to follow the group to their next destination.

When the tourists stopped at a hotel about ten minutes away, Naunet paused near the door. She spotted a chair and sat down, grabbing a magazine to hold in front of her face as she listened, keeping her gaze lowered in case anyone noticed her. Although Naunet didn't usually spend much time above water, she was still familiar with how things on dry land ran. She traveled from time to time on the surface, mostly to visit the few old friends she had left.

When she remembered her last trip, she couldn't help smiling behind the magazine. Evelyn, her good friend Robin's soul mate, had just discovered the full scope of her powers. He'd practically begged Naunet to help Evelyn figure out her water magic, so she'd agreed for his sake. When she'd seen the very modern Evelyn was Olukun, a friend she'd thought had been lost to the world centuries earlier, Robin's request had become a true joy. Evelyn looked different than she remembered Olukun, but she'd possessed every bit of the drive and sparkle as the woman she remembered from so long ago.

It was this recent introduction to her old friend that made her wait, tucked behind an archway in the foyer, knowing better how to approach humans in the present day than she would have even a year earlier. When she received a few strange glances, she realized her hair color was still a bit much for the conservative atmosphere around her. While the skin was no longer an unusual shade, the vibrant yellow-green hair still stood out.

Closing her eyes, she concentrated. Once she was sure she'd achieved the boring, dark brown she'd been going for, she opened them and considered how best to approach the strange man who gave off the foul stench of a necromancer.

With narrowed eyes, she watched the group. Instead of one large group of friends as she'd initially assumed, they were subdivided into loose pairings.

The two women in their forties were obviously together. Both sporting similarly snappy traveling attire with perfectly made-up faces, she was certain they'd taken their time getting ready that morning, especially considering the conditions on the boat. As they laughed at something a man in the group had said, Naunet noticed they exchanged light, familiar touches almost every time one of them spoke. A couple, she surmised.

Next, she turned her attention to the man who'd made them laugh. He was blonde with blue eyes, standing beside a girl with a matching complexion. Although they didn't touch the way the two women had, they shared an easy familiarity with each other and were dressed simply in jeans and t-shirts. A brother and sister, she decided.

That left only two others in the group. A handsome man, with green eyes and black hair that fell in soft waves around his face, and a quiet young woman, with dark brown hair and a shy smile. The man awkwardly adjusted the frames of his thick black glasses as he smiled at something the blonde man said.

Dismissing him as an idea blossomed, she turned her attention back to the woman. She stood a little apart from the group, as if she was there on her own. She was pretty, but in an easily overlooked way, and though she had a kind smile, she didn't seem to be speaking as much as the others.

Considering her options, Naunet realized infiltrating the group would be ideal. It was unlikely she could find an excuse to join them at this stage of their travels, but if she could replace one of the members...

Before she could make a firm plan, the group suddenly split up, each person wheeling or carrying luggage to the staircase to the right of the lobby. She watched as the girl struggled with her luggage, falling behind the rest of the group. Making a split-second decision, Naunet raced toward her.

Holding the door to the stairwell open, she smiled brightly.

"Hey, thanks." The girl gave Naunet a wry grin. "This bag is a lot more unwieldy than I thought it would be." She looked at it as if it was a best friend who'd betrayed her. "I thought I was doing amazing to pack just one bag, but I didn't realize I'd have to carry it most of the time. If I had, I would've packed a backpack instead of bringing a wheelie."

Naunet nodded sympathetically. "I can imagine. It looks like you're having a rough time. How far is your room?" Naunet looked toward where the others had already disappeared past the first landing.

"I'm on the third floor. They couldn't get us all rooms together, so it looks like I drew the short straw. Everyone else is on the second floor."

Naunet tried to place the girl's accent, but it was unfamiliar. It was similar to Evelyn's, but not an exact match to what she recalled.

"How about this," Naunet began. "I'll grab the doors as we go if you tell me where you're from. I haven't heard your accent before."

The girl's eyebrows went up. "Really? I'm not from anywhere exciting. In fact, it's probably the least exciting place you could travel."

Naunet tilted her head, even more curious about the girl now. While at first glance she had seemed to fade into the background, once you asked her about herself it turned out she could be chatty after all.

When Naunet didn't comment, she blew a piece of hair out of her eyes as she continued to struggle with her bag then spoke again. "My name is Lena. I'm from Winnipeg, a city in the middle of Canada."

"Canada? I wouldn't have guessed. I have a friend from California and I thought you sounded kind of like her."

Lena shrugged. "Yeah, I've heard that before. Probably because most of our pop culture comes from the States," she shrugged, grunting a little as the suitcase bounced up the stairs. Spying a handle at the other end, Naunet leaned over and grabbed it, lifting the back end.

Lena shot her a surprised but grateful look. "Hey, thanks. You don't have to –"

Naunet shook her head. "I know. But I figure this way, you'll be able to breathe enough to tell me more about yourself while we climb the stairs. I've never met anyone from Canada before. Is it as cold as everybody says?"

Lena laughed. "Well, yes and no. January isn't much fun, that's for sure. But it gets pretty hot in the summer." She gestured with her free hand around herself. "Almost as hot as it is here."

Naunet's eyebrows shot up. "What brings you here then? If you're from somewhere so boring?" She winked to soften her words.

Lena rolled her eyes. "I just finished my undergrad. I've always loved art history and I thought, what better way to celebrate before I start my master's than by taking a trip to Egypt and the Holy Land?"

Naunet smiled politely. "That does sound fun. I saw you chatting with a bunch of people in the lobby. Are they part of your group?"

Lena nodded, keeping her eyes ahead of her as she continued up the stairs. "Yeah, I was supposed to come with my best friend, but she couldn't make it. She had to cancel at the last minute due to a family emergency. So, I came by myself. There's no way I was going to miss this trip." She turned to give Naunet a sad look. "We've got less than a week left, which sucks. It's really flown by. I only wish I could stay longer."

Naunet nodded then realized they'd reached the large storm door between floors. Putting her end down, she pushed it open as Lena passed through. Two doors down, she stopped, looked at her key, then at the door. She unlocked it and smiled. "Well, this is my stop. If you're ever in Canada, look me up!"

"I will. I'm curious to see what 'the most boring place in the world' looks like." Naunet smiled, glancing in both directions, then even though she felt slightly guilty about it, she used her powers of persuasion on Lena. "You're going to let me into your room and we're going to keep talking. You're going to tell me everything about your life and what you've done on the trip so far."

Lena's previously sparkling eyes became somewhat hazy as she nodded agreeably. "Yes, come in. I'd love to tell you everything."

Naunet looked around once more, feeling ashamed of herself, then followed Lena into the hotel room and shut the door behind them.

Chapter 3

Naunet felt awful. She tried never to use her powers against an innocent human, especially someone who she'd have enjoyed getting to know for real. But the risk of a necromancer on the loose, potentially reincarnating the dead or stealing a god and trapping it in a human body was too powerful to ignore.

She'd seen it once before during her fight with Kek and Kauket and knew without a doubt it wasn't something that should ever happen. It was always in order to control the world, or something else similarly evil. She thanked the creator for her friends once again, remembering how the battle had raged with darkness almost overcoming the light.

Shivering, Naunet shut the door behind her and surveyed the room. Lena stood in front of her, looking more dazed now than when she'd agreed to Naunet's suggestion.

Naunet sighed. Some humans were so susceptible they needed directions for everything when they were in her thrall. Lena appeared to be one of those.

"Why don't you have a seat on the bed and tell me everything about yourself. Start at the beginning, don't leave anything out."

Almost like an automaton, Lena did exactly as she was told. She sat down then began her life story from the very beginning.

"My name is Lena and I was born in St. Norbert, Manitoba. It's part of Winnipeg now. I was born at the Victoria General

Hospital on Pembina Highway in 1996. My mom was a nurse there and my dad was a businessman for an insurance company. My best friend's name is Christina. We've been friends since kindergarten."

Naunet felt her eyes glazing over about five minutes into Lena's monologue, right around the time Lena began sharing a story from grade three. Looking around the room, she saw an instant coffee maker and headed over to see if it worked.

While coffee wasn't normally her drink of choice, staying awake all night in order to follow the boat had left her exhausted, and she still needed to listen to Lena if she was going to be able to successfully impersonate her. Lena continued to ramble as if nothing had changed and Naunet made a pot of hotel coffee while trying to listen with half an ear. After a cup and a few more years of Lena's life story, she was feeling more awake and her ears perked up once Lena reached grade twelve.

"And that's when I decided to stay close to home. The University Manitoba is a good school and it's easy to take the 170 to get there."

"The 170?" Naunet hadn't asked many questions until that point, but she didn't understand what Lena was referring to.

Lena smiled vacantly as she explained. "The bus that takes me from home to the university. Most of my classes are in the Tier building, but every now and then I'll have one in Fletcher Argue. Sometimes, I dream I'm taking a history class that I'd forgotten to show up for the entire semester. I have to write the exam, but I don't know any of the questions. And every time it brings my GPA way down."

A flicker of emotion drifted across Lena's face, but it smoothed out immediately as she continued.

"My friend, Christina, and I decided to celebrate finishing our undergrad with a trip to Egypt and the Holy Land. But then she said she had 'family issues.'" Lena paused, making little quote marks with her hands, then shrugged carelessly. "The trip has been great so far. There's this hilarious couple from the UK, two older women who totally remind me of the people from *Absolutely Fabulous,* but nicer. Then there's Amir the tour guide. He's handsome, but he creeps me out. We haven't spoken much, because there's just something about him that makes me uneasy."

Naunet nodded. That was helpful. If she were to go ahead with her plan, it meant he probably hadn't interacted much with Lena and wouldn't know many personal details or notice if she acted out of character.

"What have you told them about yourself?" She tried to get Lena to focus on the important points.

"Not much. We've been together for a week, but the Brits are so funny I mostly just listen to them. I think everyone knows I'm from Canada and my friend couldn't make it, but I don't think anyone has asked much else. There's a German brother and sister. They're nice, but their English isn't very good. And then there's Ben, who's from Australia." A faint smile traveled across her face.

Naunet knew she must be referring to the handsome man with the glasses and Lena confirmed her suspicions almost immediately.

"He's really good looking, but he's quiet too. Even if I wanted to get closer to him, he lives a world away. I'm too shy to hit on him anyway." She fell silent, staring ahead calmly.

Naunet realized Lena must have run out of life story. When she looked out the window, she saw it was already dusk. She'd been awake for close to two days and was completely exhausted. She looked longingly at the bed, deciding it was large enough to share.

"Lena, why don't you get ready for bed? Get your pajamas on and brush your teeth, then we'll go to sleep."

Lena nodded, following her instructions without question. Once she'd finished, Naunet immediately went to the bathroom and turned on the shower. Not only was she exhausted, but she was dangerously dehydrated as well. As she washed the glamour away with the water, she returned to her normal greenish complexion.

Her pores soaked up the life-giving liquid and after her energy returned, she opened her eyes, considering whether it would be more comfortable to sleep in the bathtub with water surrounding her than the bed. She measured it with her eyes and reluctantly decided against it. Not only was it too small to stretch out her tail, she couldn't chance missing the group or having Lena walk in on her in the middle of the night in her mermaid form.

If her control slipped, Lena might panic, which would cause more problems. Naunet turned off the shower, putting on a pair of shorts and tank top she'd borrowed from Lena's suitcase and reentered the room to find Lena already lying in the bed with her eyes closed.

Although she was now beyond fatigued, Naunet looked through Lena's belongings before laying down. If she was going to make a success of this, she'd need to borrow at least some of Lena's clothing, as well as her suitcase if they traveled anywhere after Luxor. But she didn't want to leave the girl completely stranded without her things either, so she settled on borrowing a pair of jeans and two shirts that were more distinctive.

Next, she examined Lena's paperwork. This part took more concentration but luckily there was a notepad beside the phone in the hotel room. With painstaking effort, Naunet made the pieces of notepaper appear to be Lena's ID then began creating sufficient money for the next day, until she could access her bank. Although Naunet was a goddess and sea creature, she'd learned centuries ago how valuable it was to have items she could access when on land. There was a bank in Luxor she normally used.

After reading Lena's itinerary, Naunet smiled. They were slated for 'independent exploration time' in the morning, followed by a tour of the museum at one p.m. and group supper in a Nubian village before the Luxor light show at night. The day after that, they were heading to the Valley of the Kings.

Abruptly changing her mind on creating cash, she focused her energy on ensuring the ID was identical to the original. Once satisfied it would pass scrutiny, Naunet stood and looked down at the sleeping girl. She hated to do what she was about to do but saw no other way to follow Amir. She concentrated on Lena's appearance to absorb every detail as accurately as possible then crawled into bed beside her and fell into a deep sleep.

Naunet woke as the sun streamed into her eyes, turning to look at Lena with apprehension. When she found her still sleeping, her heart rate settled again. That meant she still had time. The itinerary had said they were free until one in the afternoon for the museum tour, which would allow her to gather her resources.

Changing into the jeans and one of the shirts she'd selected the day before, Naunet took the hotel key from the nightstand and whispered another suggestion to Lena. Then, hopeful she'd done her best and that the suggestion would hold, Naunet slipped out of the room and headed to the bank.

Her safe deposit box with everything she needed was located at the Commercial International Bank in Luxor. After accessing the box with the key she always kept with her, she looked into the container and picked out the now-dead cell phone, as well as her Visa, MasterCard, and debit card.

She briefly debated wearing her watch or any jewelry but left them behind. They wouldn't match Lena's personality, and she didn't want them to get damaged. She hadn't accumulated many human things in her travels, but she was fond of the items she had. She caressed a mother of pearl necklace, remembering when Olukun had given it to her celebrate the defeat of Kek and Kauket, then reluctantly set it aside and closed the lid, placing everything back where it had been.

Her next stop was a store she remembered from her last trip to Luxor. As she selected clothes and a suitcase, her thoughts wandered. It was only ten, so she had plenty of time to implement the finer points of her plan.

As she considered the way the world had changed since she was young, she knew humans needed all the help they could get when it came to magic and hardened her resolve. She hated hijacking Lena's vacation, but it was the best way to keep her, and everyone else, safe from an unspeakable evil.

Chapter 4

On her brief shopping trip, Naunet found a few pieces of clothing which approximated Lena's style closely enough a casual observer wouldn't notice. And then, the real magic began.

Using the power of suggestion, she planted the thought in Lena's mind that she was suffering from a horrible migraine and needed to stay in bed until tomorrow. As the itinerary for the day involved a museum, followed by supper in Aswan and the evening show at Karnack Temple, they'd be spending another night in Luxor. The following morning, they were leaving at four a.m. for a day trip to the Valley of the Kings.

This meant Naunet had to ensure Lena didn't try to catch up with the group at any point prior to them leaving Luxor for good. Once the trip to the Valley of the Kings was over, the tour group would depart for their next destination beside the Red Sea. If she hadn't stopped Amir by then, she'd have to replace Lena for the rest of the tour.

Naunet scrutinized herself in the mirror, turning her head from side to side to ensure her complexion was the right color, and that her hair, eyes, and features matched Lena's as exactly as possible. It was challenging, but Naunet had to make sure others had no doubt she was Lena in order to stand a chance at fooling Amir.

Taking a deep breath, then swallowing two big glasses of water, Naunet exited the room to join the group. It was time to see if she could pass the first test.

As she descended the stairs to the lobby, it struck her she hadn't spoken to anyone other than Lena in a long time. Suddenly nervous at the idea of meeting new people and being expected to travel with them, she thanked the creator that Lena seemed to be a quiet person. Maybe her own awkwardness would be less noticeable. To calm herself, she ran through the information she had about the others in the group.

Ben was the engineering student from Australia who Lena thought was cute but hadn't spoken with much because she was too shy. Lisa and Ralph were the German brother and sister backpackers. Amir was the tour guide Naunet was following, with the darkest aura she'd ever seen. The couple from Britain, who reminded Lena of the actresses from *Absolutely Fabulous* were Lori and Pat.

She'd had Lena explain the reference and when she still hadn't understood she'd made her look it up for her on YouTube. If they were half as entertaining as that she couldn't wait to meet them.

When Naunet arrived in the lobby, wearing the small purse Lena used for day trips as well as her sturdy walking shoes, she was the first one there. Looking around to make sure they weren't somewhere else, she shrugged and sat down in a comfortable chair near the one she'd observed the group from the day before. The next person to arrive was Ben, who flashed her a quiet smile before sitting down in the chair across from her.

"Did you enjoy your morning?" He tilted his head, speaking with an intriguing accent.

Naunet looked down as an unfamiliar warmth flooded her cheeks. She was surprised by her reaction to him but quickly regained control and smiled back.

"It was nice. I slept in then walked around Luxor a little. It was interesting to see the differences between here and Winnipeg."

Ben laughed. "I'm sure it's quite a bit different. It's very different from anywhere I've been as well. I'm sure looking forward to tonight."

For a moment, Naunet wondered if there was something she didn't know, a subtext of some sort. Had he planned something with Lena? Then she remembered the evening light show at the Temple of Karnak and nodded briskly, trying to hide her hesitation.

"It sounds absolutely amazing, if maybe a little more Hollywood production than old Egypt..."

Ben shrugged. "I think this entire place is built on production. If it wasn't for all the old temples and mummies and stuff like that, probably a good quarter to half of the economy of Egypt would dry up like the Sahara overnight. The ancient Egyptians are making good coin for their descendants. It's right decent of them."

Naunet thought about his words and was surprised to find she agreed. She remembered seeing everything when it was still new and compared it to the present. It was true things weren't in as good a condition as they had been back then, but in some ways, they were almost more beautiful. Before she could respond, the British couple joined them.

"I'm looking forward to seeing the museum, as well as the island." The shorter, blonder of the two women spoke as they approached.

Naunet racked her brain for the name of the woman. Lena had spoken of them interchangeably, so she wasn't entirely sure which one was which until Ben gave them a welcoming smile.

"Morning, Lori. Me too." Ben looked at the brunette. "What about you, Pat? What are you looking forward to the most?"

Pat sighed, putting her hand over her heart as she fluttered her eyelashes. "As much as I'm looking forward to the light show tonight, my true love lies in the Valley of the Kings tomorrow, I'm certain of it."

Lori rolled her eyes then stared at Pat. "I thought *I* was your true love?"

Although Naunet could tell she meant it to be a joke, there was a kernel of truth hiding in the laugh lines beside her eyes.

Suddenly, Ben cleared his throat and stood up. "Ladies, how could anyone ever compare to either of you? Even the Valley of the Kings cannot compare to such beautiful English roses."

It was Lori's turn to blush. Ben's sudden rescue of the conversation surprised Naunet. She'd almost missed the brewing trouble, but if she didn't know better, she would have thought Ben had somehow seen the pain Lori had been hiding underneath her smile. Narrowing her eyes, she considered him again, trying to look beyond his quietly handsome face.

Hmmmm, he's far more observant than the average male. She focused on whether or not he had power, but as hard as she tried, she couldn't sense anything beyond a human aura. It was soothing but hardly out of the ordinary. *Oh well, at least it isn't like Amir's.*

A few seconds later, as if she'd summoned him with her thoughts, Amir joined them. Naunet forcibly held back a shudder. She needed to hide her emotions better if she hoped to get any information from him. If he *was* a necromancer, he would be cunning as well as unconcerned about disposing of someone who was inconveniencing him. Even as he emitted a darkness she could see clearly, outwardly, he remained charming and urbane.

"Excellent, I see the entire group is here. Our van is waiting outside. First stop is a quick lunch, then the museum, then a short few hours to receive a special treat- supper at a traditional Nubian village."

Lori and Pat murmured excitedly while the Germans looked confused. Ben merely waited for everyone to follow Amir out, gesturing for Naunet to walk ahead of him. Trailing along, she did her best to stay back as far as Ben would let her with his chivalry while remaining inconspicuous. Relief her disguise seemed to be holding carried her through lunch and the museum tour.

Amir drove them along the Nile in the tour van afterward. The scenic route took them from Luxor to Aswan, with their supper destination a place called Elephantine Island. It formed part of the city of Aswan and at one time had served as the border between Egypt and Nubia, acting as a line of defense between the two on the Nubian side. After a short felucca ride, the flat-bottomed boats which were so common along the Nile, they landed on the island where they were given a tour of the archaeological site.

The place seemed somehow apart from the ages, and a wave of nostalgia flooded over Naunet. She'd never spent much time on land, but this reminded her of days long ago.

If she closed her eyes, she could almost see the white rocks standing proudly beside the ocean as feluccas sailed by. Instead, the walls of buildings were made with rock that was now crumbling, and the temples and civilizations from that era had already vanished into the desert sand, leaving only the ravages of what had once been behind.

Amir led them to a small house decorated with a mural of boats along the Nile and opened the door. There, they were greeted by two women dressed in vibrantly colored fabric who gestured for the group to follow them into an open room with a lovely view of the river.

The day was warm, but the open style room captured a refreshing cross-breeze off the water, which served as a pleasant reprieve from the sun. They seated themselves on the floor as directed by a middle-aged woman with shiny, ebony skin, then two similarly dressed older girls with bright smiles began to bring food.

Amir translated what the women were saying, although Naunet could understand them perfectly well. She wished she could speak with them, ask them about their lives, but that would most certainly blow her cover as a young Canadian woman.

A cute little girl, no more than about four or five, suddenly peeked through a doorway, staring unabashedly at the strangers in her midst. Her childish giggles were audible even past the hand covering her mouth.

Naunet couldn't help but smile at her curiosity and lack of fear. When she glanced at the others from the group, she could see the rest felt the same as they smiled back at the girl.

All except for Amir, who looked bored. In fact, he was surreptitiously checking his phone before eventually placing it face down on the table. The dark magic in his aura hovered around him like a shadow, but he said and did nothing she considered alarming other than to exist, his mere presence a dark rain cloud over the day. They finished their meals, thanking their hosts profusely for the delicious bird soup and vermicelli-style noodles then followed Amir into what turned into a small marketplace in the center of the Nubian village. Naunet had the strange, prickling sensation of someone watching her and spun around.

It was the same little girl from the house; only this time, she wasn't laughing. She appeared frightened and on the verge of tears, if unharmed to the naked eye. Naunet cocked her head to the side, wondering what was wrong. Amir was walking in front with others in the group, so she knew it wasn't something he had done. Before Naunet could act, Ben, who'd been walking quietly beside her, crouched down to the girl's level and held out a hand.

Naunet knew Ben wasn't able to communicate with the girl in her language, but something about him soothed her. With a series of hand gestures and facial expressions along with a few words of broken Arabic he'd picked up on the tour, the girl stopped crying and looked at him with wide, hopeful eyes. Naunet didn't want to give herself away, but she couldn't let the little girl remain upset.

"I wonder if her mother was one of the women who served us lunch today?" Naunet deliberately kept her voice soft as she slowly drifted closer to Ben.

Ben, who'd remained crouched down, squinted up at her thoughtfully. "You're probably right. Do you have any idea where they went? I mean, if they were still back at the house she wouldn't have gotten lost, don't you think?"

Naunet nodded, pursing her lips. "Maybe they came to the marketplace when we left. I'm wondering if she followed them here and lost them somewhere in the crowd." Naunet gestured at the narrow aisles and the abundance of people milling around.

Ben stood and offered the little girl his hand. "Would you like to come with us? We'll help you find your mom."

But the little girl looked confused. She didn't appear to understand what he'd said even if she wasn't scared of the strange man extending his hand to her.

Naunet bent over and whispered into her ear in Arabic, hoping it was quiet enough Ben wouldn't realize what she'd done. "Hey, little one. This guy doesn't speak your language, but he's pretty nice. We can help you. Did you lose your mom? Where was the last place you saw her?"

Her eyes went wide and a split second later a smile broke out over her face. Ben watched with bemusement as she rattled off a stream of sentences while Naunet pretended not to understand. Once she'd finished, Naunet turned to Ben with a shrug.

"I think you're right, Ben. Her mom probably went to get something from the market. She seems willing to come with us though, so at least we can look for her together and keep her safe."

Ben looked eager to help before a shadow crossed his face. "What about the rest of the group? I don't want to get separated from them."

Naunet winced. "That's a good point. Why don't you run on ahead and let them know we'll catch up? I'll stay with her while you arrange a meeting place in a half hour or so."

Ben nodded once, then jogged over to where they'd seen the others disappear around the corner ahead of them. This allowed Naunet to use his absence as a chance to speak frankly to the girl, without the others discovering she could speak Arabic.

"What's your name?"

The girl smiled. "Keisha. How do you know my language?" She cocked her head to the side, looking at Naunet like a bird, her eyes wide and alive with curiosity.

Naunet bit her lip, wondering how much to tell her. Given her age, the magical, true explanation would probably make the most sense, and adults were unlikely to believe her even if she told them.

"Well, you can't tell anyone because it's a secret, but I'm actually not who that man, Ben, thinks I am." She leaned closer, lowering her voice to the barest of whispers. "My name is Naunet. Have you heard of me?"

When Keshia shook her head, Naunet found herself briefly disappointed. "It's okay; I don't think many people have. At least not lately. I guess you could say I have magic. Part of my magic is the ability to look like other people and to know things other people don't. I'm trying to catch a bad man but before I do that, Ben and I would like to make sure you get home safely to your mom. What's her name?"

The little girl smiled. "Her name is Zhuri. She was the lady with the blue dress at the meal today."

Naunet nodded. "That's good. What does your mother usually do after feeding tourists like us?"

Keisha thought, tapping her small chin with one finger before answering a few moments later, appearing pleased with herself. "She usually goes to buy more food for the next meal time."

"That's perfect!" Naunet smiled at the little girl. "That means she should be close by."

Keisha's face lit up. "You're right!"

Naunet leaned over the girl, tapping her little nose lightly. "Absolutely. We'll wait for Ben to come back and we can look for her together, okay?"

Keisha nodded. "I liked him. When I was sad, he touched my hand and made me feel better. I think maybe he has magic, too."

Naunet furrowed her brow at the certainty in the child's voice. "Maybe you're right, Keisha. I'll have to keep my eyes on him. Maybe he can help me catch the bad man."

Keisha nodded solemnly, but before she could reply, Ben returned.

Chapter 5

They found Keisha's mother in minutes. She'd been only a few stalls over from where Keisha had been found looking so devastated. Her mother took one look at her and pulled her into a tight hug before peering gratefully up at Ben and Naunet. Gathering Keisha closely to her side she bundled up her purchases, thanked them, and left without a backward glance.

Naunet watched them go with a wistful happiness. It hadn't taken much time away from her trip, but the slight detour had left Naunet with a warm heart and more importantly, alone with Ben. When she gazed up at him, she found it unexpectedly hard to look away. She was fascinated, but this time it wasn't just due to his good looks.

He had a quality she couldn't quite read, and after Keisha's comment, she wondered if he did have magic of his own. He seemed to be one of the nicest people she'd ever met, but he had also emanated kindness strongly enough to soothe a stranger, something that was unusual, especially for a young man. Ben didn't seem to notice anything amiss about the way she was looking at him, for which she was grateful.

After a few more moments of awkward silence, Naunet cleared her throat. "So, umm, where are we meeting the others?"

Ben gave her a half-smile. "Amir told us to meet them in a half hour at the van. He was giving everyone a chance to look around at the market items before heading back to Luxor."

"That's... nice of him."

Naunet heard the lack of warmth in her voice but was unable to disguise it. Even the thought of Amir bothered her now. The dark magic swirling around him needed to be dealt with immediately, before he had a chance to wreak any damage to the fragile balance. The thought maybe he'd already done unspeakable things turned her stomach and she stumbled on a loose stone.

Ben swiftly placed his right arm around her back, catching her almost before she'd lost her balance. Although surprised by his touch, she was grateful for the warm, strong arm around her. She was shaking unexpectedly and realized she hadn't had enough to drink at lunch.

Her human form wasn't difficult to assume, but she required far larger amounts of water than an ordinary human needed to stay healthy due to the nature of her abilities. Thinking back to what she'd had to drink at the house her heart sank. She'd only had one small glass of tea. Not nearly enough.

Ben's arm gave off another pulse of warmth. Was it just her imagination, or did she feel a little better? She shot him a smile.

His handsome features were drawn in lines of worry and his eyebrows rose. "Are you okay? You look...kind of pale." He narrowed his eyes as he examined.

Naunet placed her left hand on her neck at his expression, relieved when she couldn't feel her gills. Her glamour was holding, but she needed water, and soon.

"I'm a little dehydrated, I think. I'm not used to the heat."

Her voice was irritatingly faint, and she cleared her throat, hating how vulnerable the dryness of the desert made her. Sometimes even weaker than an ordinary human.

Ben kept his arm around her, protectively guiding her to a nearby ledge underneath the shade of a palm tree where she sat as he purchased two bottles of water from a nearby stall.

Accepting the water eagerly, she drank the first bottle down in one long gulp. His eyebrows shot up, but instead of commenting, he handed her the second bottle. This time, she sipped it slowly. When both bottles were gone she exhaled, grateful to feel more like herself.

"Thank you. I didn't realize how much I needed that." She caught his deep green eyes searching her face and stopped, mesmerized by their depths.

It's almost as though I can see into his soul, and his soul is beautiful.

Stunned at the strange thoughts in her head, she rubbed her face in an attempt to clear them away. "I think we'd better go find others," she said, standing carefully while Ben watched her with concern. "I'm fine, really."

Ben shrugged then stood up as well. "As long as you're sure. It sounds like we've got a long day ahead of us still. We have the light show tonight as well. Did you want to go back to the hotel instead?"

Naunet shook her head, not wanting Ben to say anything to the others, especially Amir. "No, I'll be fine. I should buy a couple more bottles of water though, just in case." She gave him a half smile. "I'd hate to become dehydrated again."

Ben nodded, still looking at her skeptically, but before she had time to say anything else, he went ahead and purchased two more bottles.

"There. That should keep you for a while. Did you need help walking?"

Naunet shook her head, strangely sad she'd lost the support of his arm. She couldn't justify having him carry her out, but she missed the way it felt to have his arm around her. It had been far too long since anyone had cared about how she was doing.

As the ever-present feeling of solitude washed over her, a curious thing happened. Ben reached over and casually took her hand. Just like that, her despair vanished. Naunet blinked at him as a shy smile spread over her face. Leaving her hand comfortably in his, they walked back to the van in silence.

———◉———

THE REST OF THE LATE afternoon and early evening was spent in the van. It was a quiet ride back to Luxor with minimal conversation, as everyone was full of food and tired from walking in the heat.

Amir was pleasant but distant, the same dark magic clouds roiling in his aura whenever Naunet looked his way. She did her best to act how she thought Lena would, but it was difficult. To her surprise, it wasn't only because of her fear of Amir and his magic. After her experience in the market, Naunet was also finding it impossible to keep her eyes off Ben.

Her eyes flicked over to him again. He was seated beside her, close but not touching. She was certain he was more than what he seemed to be although what exactly, she had no idea.

She convinced herself it was only curiosity making her notice the lighter brown streaks in his nearly-black hair, or the way the green of his eyes reminded her of the waters of the Mediterranean.

They drove right to Karnack temple, arriving about an hour before the light show began in order to take a brief tour. Naunet was surprised to find it was truly incredible. She wasn't sure what she'd expected, but the yellow florescent lights spotlighting the ancient structures provided an intriguing juxtaposition between the past and present.

Her eyes were drawn back to Ben, lingering on his face for a moment. She suddenly wished she could share her thoughts about the incongruity in front of them. Just as she considered moving closer, her eye was caught by a moment to her left. Amir was slipping away through the crowd. She jerked her head toward him as Ben smiled, giving her arm a gentle nudge with his elbow.

"Pretty amazing, isn't it?"

Naunet nodded. Her frustration at being stopped warred with an equally strong desire to share the moment with him. "Yes," she said, searching for words to convey her awe. "It's incredible. It's too bad the show isn't longer."

Ben shrugged. "Yeah, but it's probably a good thing it isn't. If we're supposed to get up at four a.m. tomorrow morning for the convoy to the Valley of the Kings, we need to head to sleep as soon as possible."

Naunet thought how much she wished she could sleep in the bathtub. After the bout of weakness she'd experienced today, maybe she should. So far, Lena had been very susceptible to persuasion and was unlikely to get up for anything other than what Naunet suggested. It might help her start the day as hydrated as possible, which considering the lack of humidity in the valley, was an important consideration. Suddenly looking forward to getting back to the hotel and into the bath, Naunet squinted in the vicinity of Ben's shoulder to see if she could spot Amir.

Ben turned as well, drawing his eyebrows together as he followed her gaze. "What are you looking for?"

Naunet attempted to sound nonchalant. "I thought I saw Amir leave. He was just behind you a moment ago, but I can't see him anymore."

Ben made an odd sound, kind of a cross between an interested hum and a disgruntled humph.

"Is it just me," he asked, his voice barely a whisper. "Or is Amir not the best tour guide? I mean, don't get me wrong, we haven't gotten lost or anything. He just doesn't seem to actually like people." Ben raised an eyebrow.

"You could be right. He's on his phone a lot and he keeps himself apart more than I'd expect. Then again, I've never been on a tour before. Maybe that's just how they are."

Ben shook his head. "Nope, I've been on tours before. Usually the tour guide won't shut up. At first, I liked that about him. But, I wouldn't mind actually learning *some* history about the places we're seeing. I'm starting to think I should buy a guidebook."

Naunet was trying to decide how to answer when Amir returned and addressed the group.

"The show is over for tonight. Did you want to look around further, or go back to the hotel? Tomorrow will come early, so my recommendation would be to head to bed as soon as possible. Nightlife in Luxor this time of year isn't worth losing sleep over, especially when you have the impressive Valley of the Kings to look forward to."

The group crowded around him as Naunet hung back. Lori and Pat gushed about how much they enjoyed the show, while the German siblings spoke quietly to each other. If Naunet wasn't mistaken, they were arguing but trying to keep their voices down.

She bit back a smirk. If she hadn't known they were brother and sister, she would've guessed after watching them interact tonight.

A few minutes later, they unanimously decided to head back. Naunet listened as the others described their favorite part of the day in detail. She caught Ben giving her a sidelong glance but turned her head before she could read his expression. She didn't know what to do about him; so for now, she was going to pretend there was nothing to see.

As soon as they arrived at the hotel, they broke into separate groups and made their way to the rooms. It was late, and everyone was eager for The Valley of the Kings in the morning. But instead of going to her room on the third floor, where she hoped Lena was still waiting contentedly, Naunet fell back, hiding behind the first floor doors where she couldn't be seen from the lobby.

Amir hadn't gone upstairs with the others. She was certain he was planning something and her suspicion was confirmed when he looked around surreptitiously then headed out the door into the night.

Chapter 6

The instant Amir reached the lobby doors Naunet reversed course, rushing down the stairs to follow him. It was completely dark outside by now but the energy emanating from him swirled around him, leaving a trail that was easy for her to pick up even when he disappeared from sight.

He was headed east along the riverfront and she crept along behind him, trying to make herself as invisible as possible. She relaxed slightly when he didn't seem to notice her but had to jump behind a palm tree next to a bench when he stopped walking unexpectedly to pull out his phone.

Whatever he saw angered him, and the perpetually bored expression she'd become accustomed to was erased by a black rage, which caused his face to match his aura for the first time. If she'd harbored any doubt about the nature of the magic she'd been sensing, it vanished in that instant.

His head jerked up and she ducked behind the tree, holding her breath until she realized he was staring at something over to her right. When she turned, a small Lada taxi was waiting. Before she could move, Amir strode over and leaned down to speak with the driver. After a moment, he got in and they drove away.

"Chaos take it!" Naunet cursed, whirling with a squeak when a hand dropped onto her shoulder.

For moment, she thought Amir had somehow doubled back to surprise her. When she saw Ben's calm and curious face instead, she was even more taken aback.

"Is everything okay? I saw you leave and wanted to make sure you were safe. Amir told us it wasn't a good idea for women to walk around alone after dark."

Ben took his hand from her shoulder and stuffed it into his front pocket of his jeans, giving her an apologetic look. "I'm not trying to be sexist; I just wanted to make sure you were okay."

Naunet looked into his worried eyes. An unexpected trickle of warmth spread in the vicinity of her chest. It was odd—suddenly her insides felt a little too big. She blinked as she processed his words. Was she supposed to be upset? Why? It was hard to be upset as she gazed into brilliant green eyes full of worry for her.

"I am, thanks. I mean, no. Everything's fine, I just..."

Naunet shifted her gaze to the place Amir had left in the cab. Her disappointment melted away when Ben took a step back, giving her a chagrined smile.

"I'm sorry, I didn't mean to interrupt anything or upset you. If you're busy, I'll just..." He pointed his thumb over his shoulder in the direction of the hotel and turned to leave.

Naunet put her hand on his other arm. "No, it's not you. I'm just..." she stopped, narrowing her eyes. "How did you know I was upset? I thought I was hiding it fairly well."

In the lamplight along the river walk, Naunet could see his face redden for the first time. He bit the inside of his lip, looking down at her hand on his arm. Then, as though he'd made up his mind, he gestured to the bench beside them.

"Let's sit down."

Now intrigued, Naunet followed him. She sat down half a foot away, turning her knees slightly so she could face him. He seemed uncomfortable, but she wasn't sure why until he began to speak.

"I'm not sure how much you know or believe about...people who have special abilities."

He looked at her nervously, but when she nodded for him to continue, his shoulders relaxed.

"Don't get me wrong, I'm a normal guy. I'm an engineer, like my dad, but I inherited more than just my coloring from my mum's side."

Naunet drew back, her forehead wrinkling with confusion as she considered his words. "So your big secret is that you've inherited your dad's interest in engineering, but take after your mother in appearance?"

"I'm explaining this wrong."

He sighed, running a hand through his wavy black hair, which caused a few pieces to stand on end. Naunet wanted to brush them down. With difficulty, she forced herself to focus on his words instead.

"My mum's not exactly...normal. I like to think I'm a standard geek because of my dad. But my mum has a few abilities that go beyond his knack for computers."

His eyes darted from right to left as he avoided her curious gaze then he looked down and rubbed his chin. "You could also say she's a lot older than my dad."

He searched her face while he waited for her to reply. As they stared at each other, Naunet tried to process what he was telling her. He thought he was human, but could he be saying his mother wasn't?

"All right, let's say I believe you. Your mother isn't quite human and you've inherited some of her abilities. What exactly are they?"

Ben's gaze slid away again. "You'll probably say it's nothing. I mean, hardly anyone even notices. I guess you could say I'm an empath. I can feel other people's emotions. Sometimes, that allows me to help them." He shrugged. "I'm nowhere near as powerful as my mum, but that's okay. I like being human, and I have to live in the human world. It's nice to have a skill that doesn't interfere too much with my daily obligations."

His embarrassment had been replaced by a kind of calm acceptance, which impressed her. She had a hard time with her differences, so she knew it wasn't easy. But with his skills? Living around other people would be even more challenging.

"Doesn't being an empath get hard after a while? I mean, being around other people and feeling everything they do must be rough."

Ben let out a short bark of laughter. "It can be, yes. However, in the engineering world things are a little more...well, let's just say there's not a lot of emotion most days." He smiled mischievously, adding, "I'm not sure some of the guys I work with even have feelings. Or at least, if they do they've learned how to bottle them up at the workplace. It's a pretty nice combination, to be honest. Math and science, with emotion on the side. Over the years, I've learned how to control my abilities so they don't overwhelm me. Being in the world of engineering means things are more logical and less driven by feelings. I don't need to worry about being flooded on an average day."

"That sounds pretty handy." Naunet agreed. When Ben fell silent, she realized he was hoping for more of an answer. "So, if you inherited your ability to sense emotions from your mother, who or what is she?"

Ben's uncertainty returned as he looked into her eyes. She knew he was taking a chance divulging his secrets, but spilling those of another person was potentially even more dangerous. There was power in names, and this kind of information could be used against him or his mother if he told the wrong person. But when he answered, she knew he trusted her; somehow, something about Naunet must've convinced him it was safe.

"My mum's name is Charis."

"Wait, Charis? Do you mean the one from Greek mythology?"

Ben looked impressed. "Yes, you've heard of her?"

Naunet nodded slowly. If Ben was Charis's son, perhaps he could help her after all. She was one of the Graces. Many of the Greek pantheon weren't altogether decent, but Charis was. Perhaps that explained why she'd had a son with a mortal and chose to live among them.

"How did your parents meet? I didn't think Charis was real...or at least, not around anymore." Naunet stopped, not wanting to give away her own secrets.

The last she'd seen or heard of Charis was hundreds of years ago, maybe longer. So how did she end up having a son who appeared to be in his early twenties? When Ben smiled, she was struck once more by how beautiful it was, like a rainbow after an ocean storm.

"They met when my dad was working on a bridge in the Mediterranean. They never told me the details, just that the first time she saw him, my mum recognized something extraordinary in my dad." He laughed, a deep chuckle of amusement straight from the belly.

The same strange curling warmth in Naunet's chest grew more intense. What would it be like to have a relationship like that again? It had been so long since she'd had anyone important in her life.

"What did she see in him?" Naunet didn't want him to stop talking, suddenly feeling a need to know everything about his life.

The corner of Ben's lip rose in a half-smile. "Beats the heck out of me. You'd have to see my dad to understand, but let's just say nerdy is a nice way of describing him. Even under her influence, he still hardly brushes his hair and would forget to change his clothes unless she reminded him." He rolled his eyes. "My mum, on the other hand, is gorgeous. Supermodel gorgeous. My dad still tells anyone who'll listen he can't figure out how he managed to catch her. Either way, they're still happily married. For the most part, we live in Australia; although now that I'm older, my mum convinced my dad to spend more time in the Mediterranean. She still misses where she grew up."

Naunet shook her head in wonder. How had she not known about this? Granted, Charis hadn't been someone she'd been close to, but with so few of the old gods remaining, she was disappointed she hadn't known of her continued existence. It did explain why she hadn't been able to pinpoint what was different about Ben. Empaths were often hard to read, needing to learn to block themselves off at an early age to keep from being overwhelmed by the emotions of others.

Naunet took a deep breath, falling into Ben's aegean eyes as she shared something she hadn't told a human in a very long time.

"I believe you. Your mother is one of the Greek gods, so I think you'll understand what I'm about to tell you better than anyone."

She examined his face, alert for signs of rejection or doubt, but saw only acceptance and curiosity. She was so used to being alone it was hard for her to believe it was merely chance causing them to meet now. Maybe he was part of destiny's plan for her.

Ben tilted his head. "I'm pretty open. Growing up with a mum like mine makes a guy accept things he can't always understand."

Unable to wait a moment longer, Naunet blurted put her secret.

"I'm not actually Lena."

She waited for a reaction, surprised when Ben only smiled.

"I'd kind of figured as much." He shrugged dismissively. "I'm an empath, remember? I felt something was off, right from the first time I sat next to you today. She's okay though, right? It didn't feel like you'd hurt her in any way." He looked concerned, as if the thought had just occurred to him.

"She's upstairs in the hotel room. I gave her a suggestion she wasn't feeling well, so she spent the day resting."

Ben narrowed his eyes but not with anger. More like he was trying to figure out her real appearance underneath the borrowed disguise. Naunet looked around. They were alone in the now pitch-dark night next to the river, and she briefly debated showing him her true face here, before deciding against it. There was no telling who could walk by.

"If you want, I'll explain everything back at the room and you can see for yourself that she's okay. I don't want to say anything else out here, where the night may have ears."

Ben nodded before standing and offering her a hand. "Let's go. I'm curious to find out what you're doing out here tonight." He paused and raised an eyebrow. "Of course, you do know you don't have to tell me anything, right?"

Naunet accepted his hand and pulled herself up, keeping her head high.

"I'll tell you everything I know about what's going on. All I ask is if you think you can help me, you will. Now that I know more about you, I think you're meant to be part of this."

This time when he smiled, Naunet recognized a spark of adventure in his eyes. Maybe something good would come from the dark magic she was so afraid of.

If only there was an easy way to stop Amir.

Conversation was minimal from then on. She glanced at Ben from time to time, but he seemed content to stroll in silence. As the quiet of the desert night settled around them like a thick, dark blanket, she thought how unfortunate it was her powers didn't work on land, where this battle would almost certainly take place.

With her thoughts engaged in such a way, she almost didn't notice when they arrived at the hotel. Naunet stopped nervously at the door to her room, suddenly reconsidering her decision. Ben paused behind her. "Are you sure you want to do this?" His voice was soft, understanding. "It's okay if you've changed your mind."

Naunet shook her head emphatically. "No, it's not that, not exactly." She glanced uneasily at the closed door before looking back into Ben's face, which suddenly seemed too close. "I just don't want you to think badly of me."

When she didn't say anything else, he nodded. "I know. Let's talk inside, away from eavesdroppers." He raised his eyebrows pointedly, moving his head to look both ways down the hall.

Naunet pressed her lips together, knowing he was right. Turning the key in the lock, she entered first, pushing the door open just wide enough for him to follow before quickly shutting and locking it behind her.

When she turned to look at the room, she found Lena in bed, sleeping peacefully. She wasn't sure if she'd even gotten up during the day. It was reassuring to know she wasn't putting Lena in danger, but at the same time, she had a sinking feeling Lena most likely hadn't eaten anything all day either.

She turned to Ben. "Does this place have room service?"

Ben's eyebrows shot up. "Probably. Why?"

"Lena's been in bed all day. I want to make sure she gets food before I go to sleep tonight. Should we try to fill her in on what's happening?"

Naunet bit the inside of her lip as she regarded the sleeping girl. She wasn't sure if the other woman could handle it, but Naunet was conflicted. She'd always hated taking over someone's life, even more now that she'd told someone else the truth.

Ben considered Lena for a moment, his brows drawn together in concentration. "We could," he began, dragging his words out. "On the one hand, she may understand and be fine with you impersonating her, but on the other..." he winced, turning his gaze to Naunet. "She could also have a really impressive and loud freak out."

Naunet's shoulders slumped. "Yeah, that's why I usually don't tell people anything. I just thought with how well it turned out with you..." she gestured at him before letting her hand fall despondently to her side.

Ben placed a hand on her shoulder. Tingles of warmth and comfort radiated out in little shock waves. Was that her reaction to him, or was it his power?

"I'm a little more than average though. So how about this? Instead of telling her everything, why don't you wake her long enough to eat. Then afterward, you can convince her go back to sleep."

Naunet pursed her lips. "I could do that. We had a good chat last night when I helped her with her suitcases. Maybe I could say I was checking on her because I hadn't seen her in the hotel."

Ben bobbed his head in approval. "That's good. But after we have our conversation, if that's okay? We're getting up early in the morning and I'd like to go to bed soon. Plus, I think it will be easier to explain casually checking on a near-stranger if you're the only one here."

"Yeah, that does sound more logical." Naunet agreed, sitting on the somewhat rickety office chair belonging to the ubiquitous hotel desk. "Why don't you make yourself comfortable? My story may take some time to tell."

Chapter 7

Naunet held her breath, wondering if the information she'd shared crossed the line between barely believable into the truly bizarre. Ben hadn't panicked when he'd seen her true face; in fact, she'd felt warm and tingly when he'd examined her real appearance without being shocked.

He spent the longest on her gills but had been more impressed with her coloring. She hadn't even shown him her full mermaid form, as it was too difficult to achieve inside a hotel room.

When she'd shared her suspicions about Amir and what he was up to, Ben had tensed, becoming increasingly on edge as she explained. But he didn't interrupt or ask questions until she finished. Now she sat, nervously waiting for him to say something. He finally leaned back, absently wiping his palms on his knees.

"So the magic you're sensing from Amir isn't just dark, it's a type of magic that can be used to control the power of the gods?"

Naunet nodded. "In a nutshell, yes. Although most necromancers used their power for the usual human concerns, near the end of the twelfth dynasty kingdom, the religion basically ruled everything. It was then they began to dip into more dangerous waters, pardon the pun."

A faint smile crossed his face and Naunet knew she had his full attention. Continuing, Naunet briefly closed her eyes as she remembered her fears back then.

"Luckily, few humans had enough power to unlock necromancy's full potential. By the time the Romans arrived, it had mostly faded away. The last I heard of it was at Philae in 450 BC, so to feel that same evil now, so long since I'd thought it had vanished, is terrifying."

Ben's expression became pensive. "Now you're worried Amir's planning to bring it back. Not that I'm doubting you, but where's your proof? I mean, why do you think he's planning something at that level of badness?"

Naunet shrugged, feeling helpless. "It's not something I can prove. It's more because I've seen this before I can recognize what's coming. Nothing good has ever come from this kind of darkness. I was trying to follow Amir tonight when you found me, but he disappeared."

She ran her fingers through her hair in frustration. "He took a taxi somewhere. For all I know, he could be casting dark spells right now."

Ben wrinkled his nose. "Well, we're going to the Valley of the Kings tomorrow, which will take the entire day. As our tour guide, he'll be with us. If he sneaks away, we can follow him together."

When Naunet narrowed her eyes, he held up a finger, stopping her before she could object. "No, you've already said your powers are weak on land, which I saw for myself on Elephantine Island. For all you know, I could be stronger than you are there, which is kind of alarming." He winced at the thought. "I'm sure your power is strong near the water, but the Valley of the Kings is in the middle of the desert. Maybe I'll be able to prevent you from crashing again."

Naunet reluctantly had to agree with his assessment. "That makes sense. I don't like it, and I don't want you to be in any danger, but you're not wrong."

Once again, she was frustrated by her lack of ability to do much on the dry areas of the planet. It would be so much more convenient if there was more water in Egypt. Even in places with a humid climate farther away from the ocean she had more power.

Stupid lack of humidity.

"The other reason it would be helpful to follow him together is if we get caught." He blushed and looked down. "We can pretend we snuck off for some alone time."

Naunet's eyes widened. Before she could stop herself, she felt her cheeks begin to burn. When he tilted his head up, interest spread over his face. Panic and happiness filled her at the thought of being alone with him then immediately turned into embarrassment. When she remembered he was an empath, her embarrassment multiplied.

Great. I'm falling for someone who knows what I feel as I'm feeling it. Is that a good thing or a bad thing?

"So, what do you think?"

Naunet wasn't sure if he was talking about spending time with him or the plan to follow Amir, but figured it was safer to stick to the main issue.

"Yes, let's do that. We'll stay with the tour group unless Amir leaves. If he leaves, we'll follow him."

Ben smiled with what appeared to be satisfaction. She tried not to read too much into it but was finding it difficult to control her thoughts when her heart was pounding so strangely.

"Okay, I should head back to my room. We both need to get some sleep." He smiled again, only this time, it was more like a smirk. "I imagine it'll take time to deal with Lena, and you may want to think about sleeping in the tub tonight."

Naunet laughed and accompanied him to the door. "You're right. I didn't do that last night, because I was worried she'd wake up. She seems comfortable under persuasion now though, and sleeping in water would be the best way to make sure I'm as charged as possible for tomorrow." She held the door open, looking into his amazing eyes as she tried to figure out how to say good night without being a giddy little girl.

He took the decision out of her hands, leaning down to brush her cheek with a soft, feathery kiss before stepping back.

"I'm looking forward to spending time with you tomorrow, Naunet." Giving her a crooked half-smile, he turned and sauntered away.

Of its own volition, her hand went to her cheek, as if to hold in the warmth of the kiss as she watched him walk down the hall. The sound of her name on his lips, her real name, filled her heart with a lightness she hadn't felt in ages, even in the midst of a darkness she worried would overtake them both.

Suddenly, she couldn't wait for morning.

ONCE NAUNET HAD LENA sorted for the night, she ran a bath for herself and climbed in. The cool water that surrounded her was the equivalent of a breath of fresh air. Her pores drank it in and her soul expanded with relief as the water wrapped around her with the most delicious, refreshing sensation ever.

She transformed and lay back, flipping her tail back and forth lazily, then allowed it to hang over the edge of the tub. Even though the tub wasn't large enough to fit her entire aquatic form, it was enough for her to be mostly surrounded by water.

For the first time since following the felucca, Naunet felt like herself again.

She returned to the thought she'd had walking beside the river with Ben. She should ask Robin for help. As an earth god, he was the best equipped to handle a dark earth magic, not to mention he'd been there for her the last time. Unfortunately, the main tenet of the world seemed to be that whenever there was good, a corresponding evil seemed to want to rise up to destroy it. She wasn't sure why it always seemed to be that way, but at least she knew a powerful earth god who was on her side.

She briefly considered trying to call him the way humans contacted each other before remembering Summerland had the crappiest cell reception, second only to the bottom of the ocean. So instead, she leaned back in the tub and closed her eyes.

Robin Goodfellow, Lord of the land, protector of the British Isles, hear me. It's Naunet. I require your assistance to prevent a new darkness from rising. I would not bother you, except the evil I fear is that of a necromancer, the dark earth magic that is my polar opposite. It is rising again in Egypt, the land where I have the least power. Any aid you can provide would be deeply appreciated but please, send it quickly. I fear the worst and know not what to do. I do not believe I am able to destroy it alone.

Naunet lay with her eyes closed long after her message was finished, wondering if her cries would be heard.

Chapter 8

Naunet dozed off, sinking beneath the silky liquid as she sank deeper into dreams. Soon, she was in a beautiful clearing, where the grass was lush and green and the trees were old, with branches that spread out and shadowed the ground. The sun was high in the sky but muted somehow, as though a haze of clouds covered it even though she could easily see the sky above was blue.

She looked down, realizing she was in human form but otherwise herself; gills, coloring, and all. Bemusement filled her as she looked around, knowing where she was and who she was waiting for with a certainty that calmed her. When the faint sound of laughter came from somewhere just behind her, she turned in time to see her old friend drop out of a nearby oak tree.

"Lovely to see you, goddess!"

Robin's cheery greeting was as sunny as his nut-brown skin, which glowed underneath the Summerland sky. A smile dimpled his cheeks and he looked older than she recalled, but otherwise exactly the same.

She tilted her head. "Since when did you decide to become adult in appearance? I haven't seen you like that in..." She trailed off, trying to remember the last time she'd seen him outside of his youthful little boy form, then hit her head lightly with the palm of her hand. "Of course. I'm sorry, I forgot you did that when Evelyn returned to your life."

His eyes twinkled. "Never fear. It's easy to get confused in dreams. Especially when something we're used to has changed so recently." He shrugged dismissively. "After all, we've known each other for thousands of years, and for most of that, I have been a little more sprightly and youthful in appearance."

Naunet chuckled at Robin's weak pun. He loved to say something barely witty then laugh hysterically to himself. It was part of why she'd always enjoyed spending time with him. But her amusement faded quickly as the reason she needed to talk to him pressed down on her.

"I'm sorry to bother you. I'm assuming I'm here now because you heard my plea?"

Robin's face became solemn. It wasn't a look that suited him, but relief flooded through her when he answered.

"Yes, I heard your plea. I had already begun to sense some of what you're worried about."

He began to pace, clasping his hands behind his back as he walked back and forth in front of her.

"Although the area this evil is rising isn't underneath my control, when you asked for help, I sent out emissaries to confirm your suspicions for myself."

He pressed his lips together grimly, stopping in front of her and crossing his arms.

"It is every bit as bad as you believe. The magic you've sensed is indeed from a necromancer. Although he appears to be early along his path to evil, he already feels powerful. I believe your fears about his intentions are well-conceived. From what my friends have gathered, it seems he intends to reincarnate one of the ancestral dark gods. This would be devastating to the balance, considering all of those who have been lost to the ages."

"What can I do, Robin?" Naunet pleaded. "I can sense his magic and could try persuasion, if you think he's human. But I'm not sure my powers will be enough. In the morning, I will head to the Valley of the Kings where there's no water at all."

"I know." He sighed, rubbing a hand over his forehead before he answered, drawing his words out. "I've thought about your options. I know someone who could help you. Zahara Khan. I don't know if you ever met her, but she's friends with Mai Larson, the dragon you taught to shift a few years back. Another one of Evelyn's elemental magic-wielding friends."

Naunet frowned, shaking her head. "No, I haven't. But if you think she'd be willing to help me, I'd be grateful for her assistance."

"I'll have a chat with her, but maybe the best way for you to get in touch would be by cell phone." He looked at Naunet thoughtfully. "I will have her call you. Where are you heading after the Valley of the Kings?"

Naunet narrowed her eyes as she tried to remember the itinerary. "I'm not entirely sure, but it's somewhere near the Red Sea. I'm looking forward to it. If nothing else, my magic will be stronger there and I'll stand a better chance at stopping him."

Robin gave her another smile, but a much more subdued version of the cheerful one he'd greeted her. "I'll give her your number. Hopefully, she can join you right away."

"Thank you, Robin. It helps to have you know this is happening. At times I wondered if I was overreacting, but if you're able to sense what I can and are worried as well, it's best we act immediately. I plan to follow him tomorrow. If I see any sign of necromancy, I'll stop him."

Robin pressed his lips together. "Be careful, and watch your back. I'd feel more comfortable if you waited until Zahara was with you, but I know you aren't going to let me tell you what to do."

She could hear a tone of regret in his voice as he watched her and smiled before glancing down, shy in a way she usually wasn't.

"Normally I would wait, but I'm actually not alone. One of the tourists in my group is an empath. His mother is one of the original graces."

Robin's eyebrows shot up and his eyes flashed with interest. "Wait, are you talking about Charis? Her son? I didn't realize he was old enough to travel by himself."

"I didn't get his exact age, but he's in his early twenties at least. He's an engineer, like his father, but he figured out I wasn't who I was pretending to be and offered to help."

Her cheeks warmed as she thought about him but she forced herself back to the issue as Robin gave her a shrewd look.

"I see. He's offered to help you out of the goodness of his heart."

He cocked an eyebrow, and she could tell his interest was growing as the blush deepened on her already hot cheeks. He finally relented and smiled.

"I'm happy to hear you won't be alone, but now I'm intrigued as well. You must tell me more the next time we meet."

Naunet grinned at the kindness in his eyes. He wasn't judging; rather, he seemed happy for her.

"Thanks, Robin. I will. I promise."

And with that, he waved and was gone.

Naunet blinked, opening her eyes to the cracked ceiling tiles of the small hotel bathroom and smiled with relief.

Help was on the way.

Chapter 9

After reinforcing her persuasion on Lena, including the desire to eat some of the food Naunet had procured for her, and this time remembering to make sure Lena would be able to leave the hotel if there was an emergency, Naunet joined the rest of the group in the lobby. She borrowed Lena's camera, with the dual purpose of taking pictures to reinforce Lena's 'memory' of the trip as well provide her with a prop if she was caught where she wasn't supposed to be.

When she arrived, everyone was present, but the room was quiet. No one was in a talkative mood, which Naunet chalked up to the early hour. The Brits were seated together on the couch, heads resting on each other's shoulders with their eyes half-closed, sipping coffees. The German siblings were napping on the floor, using their backpacks as pillows.

Ben was seated across from the sleepy couple, looking more awake than the rest of the group put together and Naunet sat down next to him, giving him a shy smile.

I'm far too old to be acting like this.

Just when she'd decided to break the silence, Amir entered the lobby carrying a steaming cup of coffee in one hand and his phone in the other. She did her best to school her features into a semblance of calm impassivity, but she knew Ben had sensed her true feelings when he arched an eyebrow slightly.

It was hard for her to pretend otherwise when the darkness emanating from Amir made her feel physically unwell, no matter how charming he was on the outside.

"I hope everyone slept well?" Amir looked at the drowsy group as he blew on his coffee then took a sip.

It was apparent from the way everyone was slumped over that it was too early for cheer, but in order to make it there and back in one day, the convoy had to leave at four a.m. sharp. Naunet glanced at Ben again, immediately looking away at the warmth in his eyes.

It was nice he knew how she felt, and nicer that she could feel him sending her strength without saying a word.

"Once we arrive at the Valley of the Kings, a special guide will take us into a few of the safer tombs. Unfortunately, it is not possible to see them all. A few are under construction and the others we are not allowed to go inside. You can take pictures, but no flash. It damages the paint. If everyone's ready, you may follow me."

One by one, they piled into the waiting van. Before long, she found herself dozing as they drove, the desert landscape lulling her to sleep as the sun crept over the dunes. She wasn't sure how much time had passed, but when she opened her eyes again, she felt Ben's shoulder beneath her cheek.

"Did you have a nice nap?"

His eyes twinkled, the corners crinkling with amusement as he smiled down at her.

Naunet blinked the sleep out of her eyes and rubbed the side of her mouth.

I hope I didn't drool.

"Yes, thank you. Your shoulder is very comfortable."

"I've been told that before." He winked without modesty then gestured to the front. "Amir just announced we'll be there in a few minutes. I figured you'd want to watch as we enter the valley."

Naunet nodded and struggled to sit up straight. Her cheek felt cool and lonely, but she tried to push the thought away as the van crested the hill into the Valley of the Kings. She blinked at the sight before her.

She'd never been here before but it was easy to see why it was such a popular tourist destination, even with the distance it took to reach from any major city. When the van stopped, Naunet got out and looked around at the desolate yet majestic landscape.

She could feel her powers sink to their lowest ebb and when she swallowed, her throat was already parched. A nudge on her left hand caused her to look down. Ben's tanned, wide hand was holding out a bottle of water. She smiled gratefully, and he winked back.

"Sam will be your tour guide while you're here."

Amir's voice cut past the buzzing in her head, and she looked over to see a short, smiling man standing beside him waving at the group.

Amir continued. "The tour is approximately two hours. We'll meet for lunch and head back once it's over."

"Excuse me, what do you mean, meet up?" Naunet was startled to hear herself ask a question, clamping her mouth firmly shut a few seconds too late.

Amir gave her a charming smile that didn't reach his ice-cold, black eyes. "I'll be making arrangements for the next portion of our trip. But don't fear, Sam is very informative and knows the area better than anyone. I'll meet you at the van, where Sam will drop you off after the tour. While I'm away, remember to stay together, be safe, and don't touch anything."

He smiled again briefly; then before anyone could ask anything else, vanished between the vehicles.

"As Amir said, my name is Sam and I'll be your guide today. I'm currently a student in Egyptian History at the University of Cairo, but I've been doing this tour for several years now as a summer job. It is my dream to one day be the head curator at the Cairo Museum. I've worked hard to learn everything there is to know about the Egyptian dynasties and the lives of the kings and queens who rest within these tombs. I'm honored to share the history of my people with you."

Sam had an open face and his eyes were lit with excitement, which Naunet imagined wasn't common in guides who explained the same objects day in and day out. For a moment, she wished he'd been their guide.

Ben quietly muttered, "we need to follow Amir. Before he gets too far away."

She inclined her head toward the group, keeping her voice low. "It looks like other people are joining us. Once the group is larger, we can slip away."

Ben nodded, then they turned and pretended to pay attention until the entire convoy was assembled into one large group. The moment Sam's back was to them, they slipped to the back of the group and ducked behind a vehicle.

It was easier than she'd thought to escape. Luckily, they hadn't lost sight of Amir. He was a fair distance ahead but they hung back until he entered an excavation site.

There was a large tarp on top, along with barricades and orange tape in front to block the way. Naunet looked at Ben with dismay and he frowned.

He leaned over, whispering in her ear, "it's a construction site. All of that stuff is meant to keep people out, but it appears Amir doesn't feel warnings apply to him. It could be dangerous if the ground is unstable inside."

Naunet shivered slightly. His breath seemed to cling to her neck, raising the folds of her gills which were covered only by the thin mirage of Lena's human throat. Suddenly, she felt as invigorated as if she'd just dove into the ocean. Lost for words, she could only nod and gesture for him to go first.

She crept along behind him, hoping he knew where to step. Walking on unstable ground wasn't something she was confident about. Ben paused, and Naunet had to stop abruptly in order to avoid running into him. He seemed to emanate heat and she suppressed a sudden urge to lean on him.

As her eyes adjusted to the darkness, she began to see the vague outline of a tunnel sloping gently away from where they stood. She nudged Ben gently, and when he looked down, she gestured with her head toward it. He nodded, and soundlessly, they advanced together into the darkness until the faint glow of light rose from around another curve in the wall.

It crossed her mind that they were descending into a tomb. With that thought, the walls began to press in on her. The air felt stale and she wondered if there would be enough for her to breath. It was dry; even drier than it had been above ground. Her skin felt painfully tight against her cheek bones.

The darkness wouldn't have bothered her without the knowledge her powers were at their lowest ebb, used to the inky depths of the ocean the way she was, but the dry air lashed out at her very being. The entire atmosphere seemed to warn her of impending doom and it was all she could do not to hyperventilate.

When Ben crouched down just before the barrier of the wall ended, Naunet followed suit, closing her eyes for a moment as she soaked in the strength he gave off in unconscious, fortifying waves. When she felt well enough to open them again, she looked over the small rocky outcropping, and her eyes widened.

From their vantage point, Amir was visible standing with his back to them. Her eyebrows shot up when she saw he was practically naked. They'd only lost sight of him for an instant, but during that time, he'd managed to disrobe completely except for a very small loincloth resembling the white linen wrappers the ancient priests used to wear, held up by a simple golden circlet-type belt.

His attire was the least frightening part of the scene in front of her. For the first time, she understood why she'd never seen his bare skin. It had always seemed normal, but without the usual coverings of long-sleeved shirt and pants, his skin was tattooed on each and every inch except for his hands, neck, and face. The tattoos were similar to hieroglyphics she'd seen on the buildings in their tour, except these were moving in the dim light, slithering across his skin as if alive and hungry.

Then her eyes fell upon a small altar. It was an ornately carved red sandstone with a reflective, mirror-like surface above it. At first glance, it looked like a small human was laying on top of the altar. When further inspection had revealed a lamb, she hadn't been as relieved as she should have been. She knew immediately nothing good was intended from the preparations in front of them.

Amir began to chant, his words echoing oddly in the cavern in a language Naunet couldn't quite understand. As she listened, an overpowering wave of nausea slammed into her, becoming more intense as his voice grew louder. Her discomfort eased temporarily when he stopped, but when he began again, the nausea returned even more violently.

It was if somehow he was stealing the last vestiges of magic she had within her. She stumbled and fell into Ben. His arms wrapped around her, holding her up even as her vision dimmed and her breath became tight. Before she could protest, against what she wasn't sure, she was lifted by warm, capable arms.

Bright sunlight stabbed at her eyes when she opened them, causing Naunet to groan and immediately screw them shut. She could feel she was sitting on something warm and wondered absently what was so comfortable.

Someone pushed a bottle into her hand, closing her fingers around it and helping her lift it to her mouth. Still dazed, she didn't object and let the other hand do most of the work.

When the first refreshing trickles of cold water entered her mouth, she swallowed lustily, draining the bottle, and moaned in protest when it was gone. Before she could open her eyes, the process was repeated. It wasn't until the second bottle was empty that Naunet was able to remember where she was and what had happened.

She took a deep breath, blushing fire engine red as she looked into Ben's worried face and realized her comfortable chair was his lap. His firm, well developed thighs, to be exact.

"Are you okay? I didn't know what to do. When Amir started doing whatever that was in there, you looked like you were about to pass out." Ben gestured somewhere behind his shoulder. "I scooped you up and got us out as fast as I could. I hope that was okay."

Naunet nodded, still shaky from witnessing Amir's transformation inside the cave. "Thank you. You did the right thing. Whatever he was doing down there was horrible."

She shuddered, remembering the way the words had sapped her strength. And the poor animal on the altar. She wasn't sure if it was dead or alive, only that the words Amir had spoken were full of dark magic.

"I think we've seen enough to know that he's planning something much worse than animal sacrifice, as horrible as that was to witness."

She couldn't help the fear that filled her eyes as she looked up at Ben. "I can't face him here, not in the desert. I had no idea how powerful he is already. And where did he get the baby lamb? It wasn't in the van."

He responded by pressing his lips together and stroking her hair as he cradled her. "We can discuss this later. For now, it's best if we rejoin the group. It's not a good idea for him to find us here. Are you okay to walk?"

Naunet nodded, knowing he was right. "I think so. Maybe if you could help me?" She hated being dependent on anyone, but there was a part of her that relished his concern.

He nodded, keeping his right arm tucked under hers as he helped her get up and supported her all the way back to the group. They'd only been gone a few minutes, and with everyone so captured by Sam's vibrant explanations, hardly anyone noticed them.

The only one Naunet saw take heed was Lori, but she appeared to be more intrigued about the position of Ben's arm than anything else. When Lori caught her eye, the older woman gave her a wink and with a knowing smile, turned her attention back to the guide.

To Naunet's mixed consternation and delight, Ben insisted on keeping his arm around her for the rest of the tour. Technically, she didn't need his support after the first little while, but she didn't object, enjoying the feel of him close to her.

The rest of the day passed in a blur, with a mixture of old relics, questions, and the comforting knowledge Ben was beside her. It wasn't until later that night when they returned to the hotel they were able to discuss the events of the day and what had happened inside the cave.

Chapter 10

Naunet awoke to the sound of her phone buzzing against ceramic. Still half-asleep, she turned the offending object over, glaring blearily at it from where she'd left it charging beside the tub. She'd felt so much better after sleeping in a tub full of water the other day that she'd been eager to repeat it after the ordeal in the desert. She felt better than she had last night but was still shaken at being so weak.

Even Ben, who was basically human, hadn't been affected as strongly as she had. It was almost as troubling as knowing Amir meant to resurrect something or someone. The big questions were who and when, and whether there was someone behind him, coaching him toward this goal.

Could it be Kek or Kauket? Was this what Olukun had predicted, so long ago? There were too many loose ends and no way to follow them other than by keeping watch over her sinister guide.

When Amir had returned with them from the Valley of the Kings, both Naunet and Ben had been relieved. He clearly hadn't accomplished his mission if he was still working as a tour guide, which meant they still had a chance to stop him. With the next destination beside the Red Sea, Naunet was hoping to have the upper hand.

It had been a while since she'd last visited the area, but she could still remember spending lazy summer days near the resort they were heading to and looked forward to diving into the sea the first chance she got.

She blinked a few times, focusing her eyes back on the phone as she read the text which had disturbed her slumber. It was from a number she didn't recognize but as she read, a smile spread across her face.

Hey!

It's me, Zahara. I got your number from Evelyn. Robin said you need a hand? He gave me the details of where you're heading, so I'll meet you there.

Oh, and I took the liberty of scouting out the area. When you arrive, look for a small fox with big ears. Looking forward to meeting you,

Zahara.

Naunet carefully placed the phone further from the splash zone before transforming back into her Lena-shaped form. Dressing quickly, she packed her luggage and made sure she had everything before she paused, gnawing on her lip as she looked at the real Lena, who was still asleep in the bed.

She had to decide. There were still a few days left of the trip, but she needed to stay with the group while somehow ensuring Lena got home safely. She packed Lena's suitcase as she mulled over her options, but when she finished, she was no closer to a solution.

With a heavy heart, she woke Lena and persuaded her she needed to return home at once. Making sure the woman had everything she needed to get back to Winnipeg, Naunet planted the suggestion for Lena to sleep in until ten. Hopefully, Naunet and the rest of the group would be safely away by then. After that, Lena would call the front desk to get a ride back to

Cairo to catch an early flight home, with Naunet's suggestions gradually fading away and allowing her free will to take over again.

She hoped she wasn't ruining the other woman's life or putting her in harm's way, but the stakes were too high to chance allowing Amir to do whatever he was planning. After placing as many memories as she could into Lena's head about Luxor and the Valley of the Kings, Naunet went to the door.

Taking one last look at the innocent who'd been unwittingly kind enough to share her life and her identity with her, Naunet promised once everything was over she'd make it up to her. Then she shouldered her bag and headed to the lobby.

———————◆———————

AFTER ANOTHER SEEMINGLY endless drive, quiet and boring except for Ben's proximity to her, they arrived at the beautiful resort beside the Red Sea, which would be their final destination for the remainder of the tour. She'd never stayed at a modern resort before and was impressed by the luxury in front of her. When the van stopped, everyone jumped out eagerly to peruse their surroundings as Amir smiled, gesturing at the resort with one hand.

"This will be your home for the next two days. Nothing is planned while you're here, other than a few optional activities. We have a table under the group name if you wish to share your meals. Lunch is at one o'clock and supper is at seven; otherwise, you may dine when you'd like. While at the resort, you can rent equipment for water sports, swim, or book relaxing spa treatments. I'll be around, but if you have any questions, please ask the concierge at the front desk. They will be happy to make sure all your needs are seen to. The only responsibility you have is to be prepared to depart at two o'clock on Thursday afternoon. That is when the van will take you back to Cairo. Do not be late."

As everyone nodded, Naunet considered them carefully. She'd become surprisingly fond of the others in the group, even though she knew next to nothing about any of them. They'd been a nice bunch of humans and she wondered if she'd miss them. Shaking her head free of the sentimental thought, she looked around.

The outdoor dining area was beach rustic, wicker chairs with cushions on top of large Persian rugs dotted around the lobby interspersed with small tables. A flicker of movement next to a palm tree caught her attention. Naunet squinted, startled at the sight of a small fox peeking around the leg of a chair. It deliberately winked an eye, and she immediately knew who it was.

Gently nudging Ben with her elbow, she pointed her chin toward the creature. He followed her gesture, looking confused at her intense expression for a moment before widening his eyes with comprehension. Drawing his eyebrows together, he stepped toward the fox. Tugging on his sleeve, Naunet shook her head slightly, and guided him toward the front desk without a word.

Following her lead, he didn't ask about the fox until after they'd checked in. They deposited their luggage in their rooms and met back at the wicker chairs once they were alone. They were dressed in summer attire, and it felt strange to be wearing a bathing suit underneath a sundress after how modestly she'd been dressed on the rest of the tour.

Her pores sang at the humidity coating her bare arms. She was invigorated by the smell of the sea in the air, as if she'd been released from a fog the moment she'd gotten out of the van. When Ben joined her, dressed in swim trunks and an open shirt with pineapples on it, she was both amused and flustered. She remembered a TV show she'd seen years ago once on a vacation and couldn't stop herself from commenting.

"With the exception of a moustache, has anyone ever mentioned that you look kind of like Tom Selleck?" She bit back a smile, which grew larger at his alarmed expression.

"What? No." He looked down, wrinkling his nose. "It's the shirt, isn't it?"

She burst into unrestrained laughter for the first time in a long while as the knot in her chest relaxed.

They sat in chairs near the palm tree and looked out at the sea. It was so peaceful she could almost convince herself it was a vacation. But then the same small fox with big ears crept out from behind Ben's chair and stood on its back legs, looking first at Naunet then at Ben. When it didn't make any other advances Naunet realized Zahara was probably worried about frightening him. Placing a hand on his arm, she tried to ignore the pleasant tingling sensation his skin created inside.

"Ben, I believe Zahara is the fox beside your chair. You remember I told you she was going to meet us?"

The question was mostly for Zahara's benefit, but Ben went along without missing a beat.

"Yes, of course. What should we do next?" He glanced at the fox but pretended to be speaking solely to Naunet in case anyone was around. "Is it safe to talk here?"

A small voice came from the fox, who'd edged between their chairs and sat down on its haunches, hidden from the view of others.

"It may be best to go somewhere more private, if we're going to discuss what I think we are."

Naunet vacillated, looking toward the front door then down again. "Yes, on the one hand I agree with you. But our guide told us he'll be 'in and out' over the next few days. I don't want to lose him. Did Robin fill you in?"

Zahara nodded, her nose twitching as her whiskers moved in the breeze. Her nostrils flared and she appeared to be sniffing the area. When her eyes widened, Naunet knew she'd sensed the same thing Naunet had.

"I can smell it. Dark earth magic, deadly magic. The one who wields it was just here. Do you have a plan?" Zahara cocked her head, looking between Naunet and Ben.

Ben answered with a grimace. "Mostly, our plan was to wait for you then stop him. We hadn't developed it further than that."

Naunet held back a laugh as the fox rolled her eyes. There was something almost cartoonish about watching a fox make such a human gesture.

"Well, it sounds like we need a better plan than that. You said you're reluctant to leave in case Amir slips by, but what are the chances of him leaving prior to nightfall?"

Naunet bit her lip. "When we were in the Valley of the Kings, he worked in the day."

Zahara bobbed her head. "Okay, so let's talk here. Tell me what you know so far."

"Not much, other than he seems to literally be covered in tattoos except for his face and hands." She shuddered at the memory. "They were almost identical to the hieroglyphics in the Valley. I wonder if he was wearing the Book of the Dead."

Ben looked at Naunet with furrowed eyebrows. "I didn't realize that's what they were. Well, whatever he was chanting made Naunet pass out. I had to carry her away before he saw us."

Zahara shot her a wide-eyed look. "He drained your energy?"

Naunet nodded, remembering how horrible she'd felt. "Yes, but I can't be sure how much of that was him versus the desert." Naunet felt the need to apologize. "My powers are weaker the farther I am from water. The Valley of the Kings is extremely dry; once Ben gave me a few bottles of water to drink, I felt better."

Ben disagreed. "If it had just been the dryness, you would've been fine. Maybe your powers wouldn't have worked. But the combination of the dryness as well as what he was saying drained you. I watched it happen and it scared me."

Zahara's ears drooped. "That isn't reassuring. If that's the case, we need to keep him from beginning the ritual, or barring that, interrupt him as soon as we can. His strength is the dark side of earth magic, so your power will be more useful against him, as long as we're close enough to water for you to be at your strongest."

"That's what I'm hoping. So far, my plan is to follow him and use Ben to sense his feelings. Anger, elation, whatever."

Zahara tilted her head curiously.

Ben smiled. "I'm an empath. I should be able to sense his emotions early enough to slow him down and help you find a way to capture him."

Zahara ducked her chin. "Got it. So is the plan to trap him, incapacitate him, or..." her words trailed off when Naunet lifted her hands helplessly.

"I'm not sure. I'd prefer not to kill him, because I'm sure he's still human. I'm also worried something or someone else is behind everything."

It was the first time Naunet had spoken her deepest fear aloud, and the look of shock on Ben's face was matched by a grim acceptance from Zahara.

"I was worried you were going to say that. You think he's going to attempt to stuff an old, dark god inside the body of a human, don't you?"

Naunet nodded slowly as Ben looked at her. She thought she saw disappointment in his eyes.

"You never said anything to me about that possibility." His voice was quieter than she'd ever heard it.

Naunet flushed, feeling she'd let him down and wanted to explain herself. She wasn't sure why it was so important to make him stop looking at her like she'd popped his balloon, but it suddenly mattered very much.

"I didn't want to say it out loud. I was hoping it wasn't true at first, but after talking with Robin, and now with Zahara here, I can't deny it anymore."

Ben sighed, clasping his hands together between his knees then looked up. The corner of his mouth turned up and his eyes softened, the momentarily disillusionment dissolving under forgiveness.

Naunet melted at the warmth.

"Well, now that it's out, your theory makes sense. When do we leave, and where are we going?" Ben tilted his head, one eyebrow raised.

Zahara turned to Naunet as well, ears perked up attentively.

Naunet smiled grimly at both of them. "As soon as we see him."

The three allies sat silently staring at each other, oblivious to the beauty surrounding them on the sunny day at the Red Sea resort. Sooner than they'd ever wanted to, they'd be facing a darkness beyond what any of them had expected to find along the Nile.

Chapter 11

Clouds descended, changing the bright daytime into something more akin to the dream state. Although the sun was still out, the atmosphere took on a hazy quality that felt ripe with portent. They sat, outwardly chatting quietly but alert, with eyes and ears open for signs of Amir or his dark aura.

They were soon rewarded for their trouble. Without looking right or left, Amir exited from the main hotel doors and cut through the lobby, across the sand, heading toward the beach at a rapid clip.

Zahara streaked after him, a blur of tan almost invisible on the sand. Naunet and Ben stood up and followed more sedately. Ben offered her his hand, which she accepted as her heart fluttered. For her, at least, holding his hand had become far more than just a cover.

Hand-in-hand, they strolled along the beach in the direction Amir had gone, following his footprints on the sand. Naunet was sure Zahara would catch up to him first, so she wasn't worried they'd lose him in the open expanse. They hung back until they could barely see his figure advancing on a rocky area about a kilometer away from the resort.

Naunet leaned closer to Ben, keeping her voice down. "Do you know much about this area?"

Ben shook his head. "Only what I've read in the pamphlets. Why?"

Naunet pointed toward the rocks, dread making her voice tremble slightly. "He's going to do something in there. If I'm thinking of the right area, those rocks contain sea caves. They're a perfect place for someone to conduct covert activities, especially on a cloudy day."

Ben squinted then shook his head, looking disappointed. "All I can see are rocks."

Naunet nodded. "I'm sure it's there. Can you see Zahara?"

"No, but I can see him, so I'm sure she's near."

"Okay, once we get closer, hang back. Once we see Zahara, we can enter together."

"Okay, if you're sure..." Ben reluctantly agreed then added, "don't you think it's better if she approaches from another way? Just in case he sees us?"

"You're right," she frowned. "Okay, when we see her, we'll stay together and signal her to sneak in behind us."

Ben nodded then conversation ceased. Naunet knew she was gripping his hand too tightly. When she saw her white-knuckled hand practically shaking, she was reminded of how she'd felt in the cave in the valley and fear rolled over her, churning her stomach and making her feel nauseated again.

Ben, sensing her disquiet, stopped walking. He looked down and gave her hand a gentle squeeze.

Naunet's eyes were wide as a soothing warmth passed through her hand and into her body, returning her to calmness.

"I didn't realize..." she heard the breathlessness of her voice and almost didn't recognize it as her own.

He smiled crookedly. "I've got a few tricks up my sleeve."

She smiled back, her spirits lifted by his energy. Not only did she feel more relaxed, she felt more hopeful too. Maybe things would be okay after all.

But when they reached the rocks, all of her confidence evaporated. The mouth of the cave gaped open, a large set of fresh footprints abruptly stopping at the stone floor that led inside. Looking to Ben for reassurance, Naunet was mesmerized when his green eyes warmed, and he slowly dropped his lips to hers.

For a moment, she swore she heard singing somewhere far away then just as abruptly, the music stopped when his gentle lips left hers. She put her fingertips on her mouth, unable to do anything other than stare into his eyes.

"That's to give you something to think about until later. You know, for luck." Ben's eyes glittered with an emotion she couldn't read.

"For luck," she echoed, a smile blossoming over her face.

He bit his lip then shook his head as if clearing away cobwebs. "There's so much more I'd like to say, but now isn't the time." He closed his eyes briefly then turned to the entrance. "We should go."

Conflicting emotions rocketed through her. Wonder, fear, infatuation, and apprehension were a heady mix. And yet somehow, that strange mixture gave her the strength to turn and walk into the cave beside him.

The darkness deepened as they crept into the cave. The walls glittered with seawater, and the smell of marine life was pungent. Naunet looked behind her for Zahara, feeling something small and furry unexpectedly brush against her leg. She almost screamed, then glimpsed the familiar bright eyes near her knee. Exhaling shakily with relief, Naunet nodded a silent greeting.

Continuing on as a threesome, they stepped quietly around puddles as the cave walls twisted and turned, narrowing the deeper they went. The dripping of water echoed, the only sound in the deepening silence until a soft golden glow lit up the end of the tunnel, casting crazy shadows that seemed to dance and sway.

Naunet pointed to Zahara, holding her hand up for the fox to wait, then counting to five on her fingers. Immediately understanding what she meant, Zahara paused on her haunches until Naunet and Ben were at the end of the tunnel, then slunk forward, a nearly invisible shadow against the others moving near the floor of the cave.

The same nausea began to overwhelm her, but Naunet forced herself to breathe. Ben's calmness helped and gradually, her stomach settled. Swirling dark magic seeped from the ground, swirling in eddies that licked at her feet.

How could Ben not sense that?

She glanced back, noticing Zahara's ears were folded back against her head, the fox clearly unsettled by what she sensed. As they rounded the next corner, Naunet had to catch her breath.

Amir was there, dressed the same as he'd been in the tomb. His tattoos crawled over his biceps as he readied a flat stone with an offering. Only this time, her heart clenched painfully.

It was a human.

Based on the condition of the clothing and hair, it looked like Amir had taken someone off the street. Most likely one of the world's forgotten souls no one would miss. Well, not if she had her way. Even though she was beginning to feel painfully ill again, she was in the position to draw on her powers now that she was close to water. She called to the sea, encouraging it to overpower her senses and block the darkness making her ill. Allowing her magic to grow, Naunet felt the swirling tingle as it flowed through her.

It became apparent almost immediately that Amir was able to sense her magic as easily as she could sense his. As she used her magic to strengthen her, Amir turned around, just in time to see her drawing the blue light of the water magic toward her.

His lip curled and he seemed to grow in size, throwing his shoulders back as his chest filled with air. "You? What are you doing here?"

Then, he saw Ben standing to her side. He narrowed his eyes, tilting his head as his gaze shifted between them. "What is this? Are you following me?"

Ben answered with a shrug, doing his best to appear nonchalant as he placed himself slightly in front of Naunet, completely obscuring the small fox.

"We were out for a walk and saw someone going into the cave. Had no idea it was you, mate. By the by, that's some sweet artwork you've got there, where'd you get it?"

Naunet was impressed at Ben's quick thinking and the way he'd managed to sound exactly like a college student casually asking questions. But while she thought it an admirable job, Amir didn't accept the excuse. It was probably a little hard for him to buy Ben's act with a human lying on an altar beside him.

"You *were* following me. Who are you, and what do you want? I'm busy right now. I don't have time for interruptions." Amir thrust his jaw out as his hands twitched, causing the dark magic to rise higher. "On second thought, I don't really care. You won't be around long enough to be a problem."

"My name is Naunet."

Ignoring the implied threat he was backing up with a dark mist that was raising, and giving up any pretense of being anything other than who she was, Naunet dropped her glamour and became the goddess she'd always been. Her long greenish-yellow hair trailed down her back, and her gills were now clearly visible as her skin glistened in the low torchlight Amir had set up in the sea caves.

Amir shook his head, looking stunned at her transformation. She could see his confusion as he tried to comprehend her appearance and realized he had no idea who or what she was. For someone attempting to recall an ancient evil, he wasn't as well versed in magic as he should be.

Emboldened by the way the darkness in his hands had sputtered, Naunet took two steps closer. She wasn't sure if the man on the altar was still breathing or not, but she kept her eyes firmly fixed on Amir's face, knowing she couldn't afford to be distracted before she stopped him.

"One day, while I was minding my own business, I came upon the stench of dark magic. But not just any dark magic; this had a particular fragrance of a kind I hadn't been confronted with in centuries. With the balance of good and evil as tenuous as it, I have a duty to ensure that whoever wields such filthy, tainted powers is stopped. Whatever you're planning, I can't let you continue."

Amir laughed, a sinister sound that echoed around the small enclosure, already over the surprise her transformation had caused.

"Tainted?" The laughter stopped abruptly as he glared at Naunet. "Someone sure thinks a lot of themselves. Perhaps if you were able to see just how impressive this power can be, you'd change your mind."

Amir swiveled, abruptly turning to face the man on the altar as he dismissed her.

Naunet knew he was about to begin chanting again. She needed to act quickly, and stop him before her powers were weakened. It was all up to her now. She looked at Ben but he'd already begun creeping toward the unconscious man, so she created a distraction.

"No!"

Her shout caused Amir to stop, glaring furiously at her as he changed directions and advanced toward her instead of the altar. This gave Ben his opportunity and he darted behind Amir, scooping the unconscious man up and throwing him over his shoulder before darting back to the entrance.

Naunet focused, creating glowing balls of water in each hand. Once they were large enough, she joined them together to create one massive, swirling globe which she threw directly at Amir. He blocked with a dark wall and the ball rebounded, splattering against the cave, harmless water once again. She repeated the process, but this time Amir closed his eyes. When he opened them next, her lip curled in repulsion.

His pupils had been entirely replaced by a solid white and his skin color had changed, with veins now prominent on his face and neck in the areas untouched by the creeping tattoos while the background had become a greyish-brown. He was chanting louder now and the familiar drain tugged at her, making her feet stick. She stumbled, almost falling over until she was caught by a familiar pair of strong arms.

She looked up, bewildered. "Ben? You're supposed to be getting yourself out, along with his offering."

He winked, lifted her chin and planted a quick smack on her lips. Instantly, her energy returned. Before she knew what he was planning to do, he'd leapt onto Amir, knocking him to the ground and getting in a few solid punches before he grabbed the man's head in both hands and held on.

Amir shrieked, a terrible, guttural sound that chilled her, removing some of the warmth Ben's kiss had restored. Ben's eyes were closed as he maintained his grip on the now thrashing Amir. Frozen to the spot as the men wrestled, Naunet couldn't stop her hand from flying up to her mouth at the sight of Ben soaring toward the cave wall, hitting with a solid thud before crumpling and lying unmoving a few feet away. Amir stood up and began limping toward Ben's prone figure.

Zahara zipped over to Ben, placing her tiny form in front of him protectively and snapped at Amir. The now barely-human appearing man looked down, lip curling in a sneer as he lifted his foot to kick her away, clearly viewing her as nothing more than a minor annoyance.

But before he could make contact, a tower of sand rose up and trapped his leg. His eyes went wide, fury filling them. He lifted the other foot in an attempt to repeat the movement, and another sand tower rose up, trapping him in earth up to both knees.

Ben stirred with Zahara's encouragement as Naunet wracked her brain for ideas and searched their surroundings. When her eyes fell on the entrance, they stopped. It could work, but only if her timing was perfect. Praying to the creator, she closed her eyes and let the full strength of her power rip through her.

A loud rumble echoed through the cave just as Zahara helped Ben to his feet. Relief filled Naunet when she saw he was moving well enough to grab onto the unconscious man who'd been on the altar. As he began to stumble toward the exit under the other man's weight, water rushed into the cave in a flash flood of supernatural proportions.

Amir's eyes snapped open, looking human again as the water knocked him off his feet. He screamed as he was flung across the cave and smashed into the far wall.

Good, serves you right for doing that to Ben.

Naunet transformed completely once the cave was submerged in water, triumph spreading as she used her powerful tail to push herself up and away from him. Listening in the now sudden and total darkness of the sea with her power, she concentrated. She could sense Zahara, swimming ahead and out of the cave into the sun and turned her focus to Ben. He was almost out, but she felt him beginning to falter under his burden.

Naunet swam to his side in a flash, taking ahold of him beneath his arm and pulled him behind her out of the cave. They burst into the glorious daylight and after swimming to the shore, she deposited Ben and the man onto the beach.

Her vision cleared to find the Red Sea sparkling innocently in the beautiful afternoon sun while three wet bodies lay on the sand beside her. Zahara sprang to her feet immediately and shook herself off, looking more like a disgruntled cat in her damp state than a fox, but appeared otherwise well. The others weren't moving, so Naunet transformed back to her two-legged form to take a closer look.

She leaned over and carefully shook Ben. Had he hit his head or inhaled water into his lungs? Had Amir damaged his spine when he'd thrown Ben off so violently?

"Ben! Are you okay?"

At her gentle jostling, he began to cough. A moment later, he turned to his side and expelled a large amount of seawater before he stopped and rested on his hands and knees. After he was finally able to catch his breath, he brushed his hair back and looked at her with the crooked grin she'd feared for a moment she'd never see again.

"That's exactly what it feels like to ride inside the tube."

When she wrinkled her brow, he gave another weak smile. "Surfing, love."

Although his words were light, and she knew it was a human expression, the moment he said the word love, Naunet felt as if she was back in the cave. It seemed like she could hear water whooshing in her ears again, and for moment, she forgot everything.

Zahara's insistent voice broke into her fog. "Amir. Where is he?"

Naunet shook her head, looking back toward the cave. "I can sense him by the faint ebb of the dark magic. He's still in the cave, under the water."

Zahara bared her teeth. "Alive?"

Naunet concentrated, but her answer was grim. "I can't sense if he has a heartbeat, and the magic is gone now as well. The water feels clean again."

"Dammit!" Zahara growled as her furry shoulders slumped.

Naunet looked down in shame. She'd failed. They wouldn't be able to ask him any questions about what he'd been doing or why. If someone else was orchestrating this, they'd lost their chance at finding out from Amir.

Ben gently placed his arm around her shoulder, his wet skin as comforting as ever. "You did what you could. His emotions were..." he shook his head, looking at Naunet earnestly. "He meant to kill all of us, you know."

Ben knelt down beside the stranger, who was still unconscious but looked cleaner from the water. Close up, she could see he wasn't homeless as she'd first assumed.

"I was able to read his emotions around the man. I caught flashes of the hotel bar, and Amir's joy at finding him after having one too many. His emotions were so dark I'm certain he was going to kill him and use the body for God knows what."

Naunet sighed, knowing he was right. The dark magic she'd followed all the way from the mouth of the Nile was gone now, washed away by the waves. But she was certain this was only the beginning. Amir had been a servant of something much darker, more powerful, and much older.

If only she'd had a chance to find out if her suspicions about the source were right. Naunet turned to Ben and Zahara and tried to put her worries behind her.

"Amir's magic is gone, so our task has been accomplished." Naunet smiled, amused at the wet and still bedraggled Zahara's hang-dog expression. "Thank you for your help; although in the end, perhaps it turned out to be a waste of time for you."

Zahara disagreed. "I'm glad I could be here. Besides, this area is technically under my protection. It was important for me to know this was happening, especially if it is the beginning of something bigger and darker. Let's keep in touch, all right?"

Naunet nodded, crouching down and holding out a hand to the fox. Zahara bared her teeth in a smile then nimbly leapt toward her, placing one tiny paw in Naunet's hand.

"I'm going to head home. I left my husband alone with the kids. He's likely already petitioning every god and demigod he can think of to help him."

Naunet laughed, her spirits lightening at the fox's dry humor. "I promise to keep in touch. Thanks again, Zahara."

Zahara bobbed her head and took off over the sand, disappearing into the distance.

Naunet looked at the man on ground, then at Ben. "What are we supposed to do with him?"

Ben looked around the beach then leaned over and grabbed the man by his shirt, dragging him further away from the water. "Best bet? Leave him here. His breathing is good and he smells like he's had enough booze to keep him foggy for a while yet. I'll roll him into the recovery position. He should be fine. Look, he's already starting to stir. My guess is if he remembers anything, he's going to chalk it up to hallucinations brought on by too much drink."

Naunet nodded, grateful for one less thing to worry about, then her eyes were drawn unerringly back to Ben.

"What about... us?"

For once, her cheeks didn't flush. What they'd been through had emboldened her to go after what she wanted. For the first time in forever, she cared about someone. If darkness was trying to reemerge from the shadows and take over the world, there was no time to waste being shy.

Ben stepped closer. Bringing both hands to rest on her shoulders, he lightly stroked them in a way that sent shivers down her back. Then, he dropped his face closer, pressing his lips to hers and answering her question in a way that was clear and full of extraordinary promise.

NOTE FROM THE AUTHOR

Thank you so much for taking the time to read my book! I hope you've enjoyed reading about the adventures of my characters as much as I enjoy writing them. I'd initially started my series with the intention to write just one book, then it turned into a trilogy, and then I created my own world. (I have issues with goodbye, apparently!)

Reader reviews are incredibly important to indie authors like myself, so it would mean so much if you could take a few minutes to leave an honest review wherever you buy books online. Even a few words can make the difference in helping a future reader give a book a chance, as every review makes a novel more visible in the vast ocean of literature.

If you're interested in receiving updates, giveaways, or advanced copies of upcoming books, sign up for my mailing list at https://www.subscribepage.com/hmgooden newsletter, or through my webpage at https://hmgoodenauthor.com. You can also follow me on Facebook, Instagram, Twitter and many other places. I always love to hear from readers and other writers and do my best to answer every comment when possible.

I hope you'll join me in my next adventure!

COPYRIGHT INFORMATION

Don't miss out!

Visit the website below and you can sign up to receive emails whenever H. M. Gooden publishes a new book. There's no charge and no obligation.

https://books2read.com/r/B-A-POWE-VWUY

BOOKS 2 READ

Connecting independent readers to independent writers.

Did you love *Darkness on the Nile*? Then you should read *Dream of Darkness* by H. M. Gooden!

Cat's used to moving, to never quite fitting in.

But when her family moves to Valleyview, she's not expecting what happens next.

A serious accident, a coma, then the real strangeness began.

Cat is faced with an entirely new set of powers as well as an ancient evil packaged as the high school hero. And if that wasn't enough, she'll also discover that her family is far more than what she's been told.

Grade 10 just got a lot more challenging.

Read more at https://www.hmgoodenauthor.com/.

About the Author

H. M. Gooden has always loved the world of books, but over the last few years a new story has begged to be told, and as a result, this series was born.

In between dealing with children and work, the majority of the actual writing happens between four and six am and involves multiple cups of coffee for inspiration.

You can always find me on Twitter, Facebook, Instagram, Bookbub and Goodreads.

I always love to hear from readers!

Read more at https://www.hmgoodenauthor.com/.